THE MAD MASK

THE
MAD MASK

by BARRY LYGA

SCHOLASTIC INC.
NEW YORK TORONTO LONDON AUCKLAND
SYDNEY MEXICO CITY NEW DELHI HONG KONG

ISBN 978-0-545-19653-6

12 11 10 9 8 7 6 5 4 3 2 1   12 13 14 15 16 17/0

Printed in the U.S.A.   40
First Scholastic paperback printing, January 2012

The text was set in Sabon.
Book design by Christopher Stengel

Also by Barry Lyga

ARCHVILLAIN

For David, who wouldn't take
"No" for an answer

ARCHVILLAIN

Kyle Camden has superpowers!

You'd think this would be great news, but nope! Kyle got his powers one night when he witnessed a "plasma storm" on the outskirts of Bouring, the town where he lives. At the same time, he also saw the arrival of Mighty Mike, a superpowered alien kid who has become a superhero and the darling of the town and the news media.

So Mighty Mike is now the most popular kid at Bouring Middle School, a role that was once occupied by Kyle. But Kyle's famous, elaborate pranks — which make adults look like fools — just can't compete with Mike's superpowers. And when Kyle tried to pull a superpowered prank on Mike — by, uh, erasing his pants with a high-powered laser — it didn't go well and chaos ensued. (Good news: Kyle was disguised as the "Azure Avenger" at the time. Bad news: Everyone calls him the "Blue Freak" instead.)

Only Kyle knows that Mike is from outer space. He can't tell anyone, though, because then they would know that he had witnessed Mike's arrival . . . and they would know that he's the Blue Freak. Kyle doesn't want people with inferior intellects mucking around with his powers, like the doctors and scientists who are always studying Mighty Mike.

(Oh, yeah — Kyle's intelligence is also off the charts. He was smart before the plasma storm, but now he's even smarter.)

Things got even worse when a dirt monster (you had to be there) tried to kill Kyle's best friend, Mairi MacTaggert. Kyle saved the day, but he did it from behind the scenes — to everyone else, it looked like Mighty Mike saved Mairi . . . and like the Blue Freak made things worse, not better.

So now Kyle has decided it's no more Mr. Nice Guy. With the help of Erasmus — his specially programmed iPod — he's going to do whatever it takes to destroy Mighty Mike. So far, that has meant lots of run-ins with the law, as Kyle tries to track down the components he needs for various gadgets that will help him to:

A) Expose Mike as an alien from another world, OR

B) Wipe the alien punk out, OR

C) Embarrass him to the point that he leaves town (and, preferably, the planet), OR

D) Some combination of all of the above.

It's not easy being Kyle. . . .

CHAPTER
ONE

"BLUE FREAK! WE HAVE YOU SURROUNDED! PLACE THE BARREL ON THE GROUND AND PUT YOUR HANDS ABOVE YOUR HEAD!"

Kyle grumbled under his breath, hovering a hundred feet over the parking lot at Axis Research & Consumer Products (motto: "Your world revolves around us!"). He counted quickly. There were sixteen Rent-A-Cops down there under him. He wasn't worried about them.

There were also about a dozen real cops. Guys from the Centre City Police Department, including the guy with the bullhorn. He wasn't worried about them, either.

Add to that a couple of FBI agents. Eh. No big deal.

But the platoon of Army guys? Yeah, *that* he was the tiniest bit worried about!

Fortunately, there were also reporters and cameramen down there. It looked like Channel Five ("Alive @ Five!") and Channel Thirteen ("Thirteen's Your Lucky Number!"). Good. Kyle liked being on TV. He was certainly more important than the usual garbage they showed.

He cleared his throat and glared down at more than fifty pairs of eyes and a couple dozen guns all pointed at him. Then he spoke through the PA system he'd installed in his mask:

"ATTENTION COPS AND OTHER IDIOTS! FIRST OF ALL, MY HANDS *ARE* ABOVE MY HEAD!" (It was true — Kyle held a barrel of extremely rare chemicals over his head.) "SECOND OF ALL, I'M NOT THE BLUE FREAK! I'M THE AZURE —"

He was cut off by a hail of bullets from below. They whizzed and sang as they flew past him.

"Idiots," he mumbled as he twisted in the air to avoid being hit. Kyle was bulletproof, and everyone knew it. They were just trying to intimidate him. But the barrel of chemicals wasn't bulletproof — those morons could rupture it and destroy the very thing they were trying to save. Plus, they might poke holes in his costume. There was no way in the world Kyle was wasting another night with a needle and thread, patching this thing. (How was it that the guys in the movies got into fight scenes every five minutes and never had to sew up their costumes?)

"ATTENTION, MORONS!" Kyle called out. "YOUR BULLETS CANNOT HURT ME!" He wanted to just fly away, but he couldn't let anyone see which direction he was flying. The authorities believed that the "Blue

Freak" was based in or near the town of Bouring, and Kyle didn't want to give them any more evidence. Or lead them straight to his house. He could just picture the looks on Mom's and Dad's faces when they opened the door to see the FBI and half the U.S. Army standing there.

The thought made him laugh out loud. Oops. He had forgotten to turn off his PA — his laughter boomed out over the parking lot.

"WE'RE GLAD THIS IS SO AMUSING TO YOU!" the cop said through his bullhorn. "HOW DO YOU LIKE *THIS*?"

Just then another wave of ammo came up from the ground. But this time, it was a new kind of ammo — smoke grenades and rocket-propelled nets. There were also some long, skinny silvery things that Kyle quickly identified as tranquilizer darts. Were these people completely brainless? If a bullet couldn't go through his skin, did they really think a dart would do the trick?

"Oh, you're *kidding* me," Kyle said (this time with the PA turned off). "Are these jokers for real?"

"Stop wasting time with them," Erasmus said through his earbuds as Kyle deftly dodged the nets and flew higher than the smoke. A stray smoke grenade came near him and he knocked it aside with an effortless kick, easier than tapping a soccer ball into the net. "We have more important things to do than to play with the cops."

"It's not just the cops," Kyle told the artificial intelligence. He had programmed Erasmus based on his own thoughts, so why did he have to keep explaining things? "It's the Army and the FBI, too. I'm not playing — I'm studying their patterns."

"They have idiotic patterns," Erasmus said. "They can't get to you from the ground." He paused. "Oh. I just intercepted a signal. They have fighter jets scrambling from an Air Force base fifty miles from here. They'll be here in —"

"ATTENTION, BLUE FREAK!" Now it was an FBI agent in shades and a boring gray suit with the bullhorn. The cop who'd had it was kicking at the ground as he stalked off. Kyle felt momentarily bad for him. "WE HAVE SUMMONED MIGHTY MIKE!"

Kyle stiffened at the mention of his nemesis. "Of course you have . . ." He seethed under his face mask.

"Cowards," Erasmus spat. (A neat trick, considering Erasmus didn't have any spit. Or a mouth, for that matter.)

"SURRENDER NOW AND HE WON'T HURT YOU!"

"TELL YOU WHAT," Kyle blared, "YOU TELL *HIM* TO SURRENDER!"

"T-minus three minutes to the jets," Erasmus warned.

"Wait for it," Kyle said, executing some more aerial

acrobatics in order to dodge the latest pathetic volley of bullets, nets, and grenades from below.

"*Kyle . . .*"

Kyle hated the way Erasmus could seem to talk down to him just by saying his name. He figured maybe it was time to reprogram the AI to call him "Master" or something a little more respectful.

"I want *him* to see," Kyle said.

And just then — as if summoned by Kyle's desire — a dark pinprick on the horizon moved and became clear.

Mighty Mike.

The do-goodingest do-gooder on the face of the planet. Resplendent in his green-and-gold costume, the cape fluttering in the wind as he soared toward Kyle, his fists ahead of him, his blond hair blown back. He looked like some kind of movie hero, but Kyle knew better. Mighty Mike was up to something here on Earth. He could just tell. He knew it deep down in his gut.

Kyle chuckled to himself. "Wait for it," he told Erasmus again. "Almost."

Down below, Kyle watched as the cops and the others scattered. No doubt they didn't want to get caught in the crossfire when Kyle and Mike pounded each other, with Air Force jets firing air-to-air missiles at the same time. There would be a lot of shrapnel dropping out of the sky.

Well, there *would* be a lot of shrapnel. If Kyle wasn't about to escape, of course.

Mike was now so close that Kyle could see the curl of his upper lip as he bore down, snarling. Kyle wished other people could see Mighty Mike like this — angry, not the infuriatingly *nice* vibe that he threw out to the rest of the world. If he could figure out a way to show people this version of Mighty Mike, they might chase the brat off the planet without any further prodding from Kyle.

Oh, well. He would have to do things the hard way. A genius's path is never easy.

"Kyle!" Erasmus actually sounded panicked.

"Don't worry —" Kyle said, making a split-second decision. As much as he wanted to make a clean getaway, he couldn't resist the chance to tussle with Mighty Mike. So even though Erasmus was screaming in his ears, Kyle maintained his position, dodging aside at the last possible second as Mike hurtled through the air past him.

"Whoops!" Kyle jeered. "Missed me!"

Mike spun around and came back, leading with a fist. Kyle ducked under it, careful to keep his grip on the chemicals. For a few moments, he led Mighty Mike like a bullfighter, constantly out of his grasp. Mike's eyes burned with rage and he snarled. Kyle wished he had a camera so that he could take a picture of this, the real Mighty Mike. Something to show to the world.

"Kyle!" Erasmus cried. "Those jets are almost —"

"Fine, fine. Razzle-dazzle."

At just that moment, from a small copse of trees on a strip between the Axis parking lot and the highway, a tiny, almost imperceptible puff of smoke rose up. A second later, a small rocket — no bigger than a large firecracker — exploded in midair near Kyle's position.

The air filled with color and light.

Down below, everyone shielded their eyes from Kyle's latest, proudest invention: laser-chaff. It was sort of like special glittering confetti, only instead of reflecting light, it also produced powerful multicolored beams that shot out in all directions. The effect was like an endless series of fireworks and strobe lights in the sky, blinding and confusing anyone who looked at it.

Kyle, of course, was prepared for the laser-chaff. He'd built special filtered lenses into his mask, so that he could still see clear as day. Everyone else, though, was either looking away or completely helpless.

Including — Kyle laughed again — Mighty Mike. As Kyle watched, Mighty Mike flew straight into the laser-chaff. He pulled up — too late — and spun around, blinded, his hands coming up as if he could claw the lights away from his face.

"Sucker!" Kyle crowed. He wanted to stick around for a while to watch his nemesis flail about in the laser-chaff, but those Air Force jets were hovering into view over the horizon. Time to burn some air and get out of here.

He flew south at top speed. Bouring was to the east, but he knew the government was probably trying to track him with a satellite. He would fly south and then — when he was sure he'd flown fast enough to outpace the satellite — zigzag to the northeast and go home. The idiots watching him fly away would think he was headed somewhere other than Bouring.

Kyle's plans didn't always pan out precisely the way he hoped, but even his worst enemy would have to admit: His escapes were pretty spectacular.

He'd figured there was a chance he'd be caught trying to steal the chemicals, so he'd concealed a rocket launcher in the trees before breaking into the lab, with a voice command to Erasmus set to fire a grenade full of laser-chaff. It had worked without a hitch.

"Forgetting something?" Erasmus asked, a little too snidely.

"Flame out," Kyle told Erasmus, and the AI sent a second signal down to the rocket launcher that opened an ampoule of powerful acid, reducing the launcher to a puddle of metal. Untraceable.

"You're welcome," Erasmus said, a hurt tone in his voice.

Kyle sighed. Why did he have to have an AI with a martyr complex?

He kicked in a bit of extra speed. A successful heist. He was one step closer to destroying Mighty Mike.

Kyle was miles away from Axis Research & Consumer Products when a figure stepped out of the trees, not far from where the rocket launcher had slowly dissolved into a pile of shiny goo. The figure was slender, wearing a long cloak. It also wore an ornate mask, carved out of ebony. The mask was as black as midnight except for a single tear made of ivory, frozen as it trickled down the cheek from the left eyehole.

In the air, the laser-chaff was still flashing and sparking. Two Air Force jets blasted overhead, scattering some of the chaff in their wake. As the masked figure watched, Mighty Mike shook his head, clearing his vision, and spun around in rapid circles before finally giving up.

Meanwhile, the ground was a chaos of cops, agents, and soldiers. No one noticed the masked figure who simply gazed up at the sky, nodded as if pleased with itself, and then melted back into the cover of the trees.

from the top secret journal of
Kyle Camden (deciphered):

Today's "heist" was a complete success. Not only did I take possession of the drum of synthetic chemical compounds needed for my experiments, but I also held off a force of police, federal agents, and soldiers, to say nothing of escaping from the scene without Mighty Mike being able to follow.

I'm getting better at this whole "supervillain" thing.

Of course, I'm not really a villain, super or otherwise. The appearance of villainy is a necessary fiction, required by the fact that the average person is too mentally challenged to understand anything beyond a simple dialectic of good vs. evil. Therefore, if Mighty Mike is "good," then anyone who opposes him must, perforce, be "evil."

Ha!

Furthermore, anyone who "steals" must be "evil" as well. This is the worst of reductive morality, but it is to be expected from the ignorant masses.

Someday, long after Mighty Mike has been destroyed and the world has come to understand my genius, I will decipher this journal and publish it for all to see. With that in mind, let me dumb down my thinking now so that my future readers can follow along:

I am not evil. My stealing is not evil. It is necessary, for I am at war with Mighty Mike.

If the rest of the world knew that Mighty Mike was an alien, I would not be acting alone. But, unfortunately, I cannot reveal Mike's origins (for good reasons, all explained earlier in this journal).

Therefore, I must find a way to expose Mike for what he is. Since people love and worship Mike, anything I do to him will be seen as "evil," until the moment I succeed. At that point, I will no longer be seen as "evil." So until that time comes, I must endure being called the "Blue Freak" and being at the top of the FBI's Most Wanted list, and all the other indignities visited upon me.

I have my standards, though. There are lines I will not cross.

I steal, yes. I admit this. However! However, I only steal things that are absolutely necessary to defeating Mighty Mike. I do not steal for myself, you see? I steal to make the world a better place.

I refuse to steal money, for example. And I would never and will never steal anything irreplaceable. The chemicals I stole today are rare, true, but they are not irreplaceable. The chemists at Axis can eventually reproduce the process in question and create more chemicals. Yes, it will take time and money, but that's what they're there for. They work for Axis to make that stuff.

Still, I have to admit. . . . Pulling off a heist like this was a lot more fun than I thought it would be. I started out doing it because I had to, because I needed the chemicals and there was no other way to get them. But around the time the cops arrived and thought they could shoot me out of the sky, it sort of became fun. Like a game.

Or actually . . . It was like a prank, really. I play pranks in order to remind people that they aren't as serious or as important as they think they are. Stealing the chemicals from Axis was really the same thing — they were foolish enough to think that they had safeguarded their precious chemicals, that no one could ever steal them. I swooped in and proved them wrong. They'll have to rethink all of their security procedures and improve dramatically.

Really, when you think about it, I helped Axis by stealing those chemicals today!

That was nice of me.

CHAPTER
TWO

Kyle closed his journal and stretched. He was in his parents' basement, which they never used, so Kyle had turned it into his own special lab and workshop. The basement was one big room that stretched the length and breadth of the house, so even with all the old junk his parents had dumped down here, there was still plenty of space for Kyle to work on his schemes and experiments. He had multiple projects going at once, including his pride and joy: a fully functioning time machine.

Well, someday it would be a fully functioning time machine. Right now it aspired to be a fully functioning time machine.

But that wasn't the only project on Kyle's agenda. Multitasking was the hallmark of genius, so Kyle decided to completely reinvent two sciences at once. He would reinvent physics with the time machine, and with the drum of stolen chemicals, he would reinvent chemistry.

"One at a time is for wusses," he told Erasmus.

"I'd just be happy if you would finally put together that wireless earpiece for me," Erasmus responded. "Half the time when you fly around, my earbuds either fall out of your ears or the plug gets pulled out or you get all twisted up in the cable."

"Fine, fine. I'll work on it."

"You could just *buy* one off the Internet, you know."

"I want to build it myself. To my own specifications."

"If I had eyes, I would be rolling them right now," Erasmus said. "Stop being a cheapskate and buy a Bluetooth headset already."

Kyle won the argument by switching Erasmus off. What had moments before been a brilliant and annoying artificial intelligence was now a silent iPod, decked out in customized blue flames.

Kyle stretched again and twisted. Ever since his exposure to the alien energies of a plasma storm, he was basically indestructible, but when he exerted himself, he could still get sore muscles. He hopped off his workbench stool and checked out the drum.

PROPERTY OF AXIS RESEARCH & CONSUMER PRODUCTS! was stenciled on the side. Under that, it said:

CONTENTS UNDER PRESSURE
DO NOT EXPOSE TO OPEN FLAME OR VACUUM

Well, no problem there. Under all of *that*:

FACILITY NO. A1265 — *DO NOT REMOVE*

Oops. Well, Kyle didn't plan on exposing it to open flame or vacuum, so he decided two out of three wasn't bad.

He spent a moment figuring out how to open the stupid thing. It would have been easy just to crack it with a karate chop, but he reasoned that having gallons and gallons of experimental chemicals slopping all over himself and the basement probably wasn't the brightest idea in the world. There was a complicated sort of locking mechanism on the top of the barrel — it looked like a credit card swiper had married a fingerprint analyzer and had a baby. Pretty difficult. Kyle figured he needed the right fingerprint and a key card to open the tap. He also figured the right fingerprint and the key card both belonged to some guy at Axis who wouldn't let him borrow them, no matter how good his intentions.

Fortunately, what Kyle lacked in fingerprints and cards, he more than made up for in brainpower. He scrounged around for some wire strippers and a spare USB cable. Within a matter of minutes, he had the lock pried open and attached to Erasmus. He switched the AI back on.

"Okay, Erasmus. I need you to crack this lock and open it up."

"How am I supposed to do that?" Erasmus complained. "In case you haven't noticed, I don't have fingers, much less finger*prints*."

"You don't need fingerprints. The lock just needs to *think* that the right fingerprint has been put on the screen. You can hack into the little computer in there and convince it that it's already seen the right fingerprint."

"That's going to be a lot of work. Wouldn't it just be easier to go get the guy with the right fingerprint? Or just get his finger?"

"Erasmus!" Kyle couldn't believe what he was hearing. "I'm not going to take someone's finger!"

"It's not like he doesn't have nine more . . ." Erasmus grumbled. His hard drive whirred, and Kyle knew that he was hacking the lock. "Don't know what you people need with those fingers anyway. I get along just fine without them."

"That's enough commentary. Just keep working."

The basement went silent except for the occasional click and hum from Erasmus's hard drive (Kyle made a mental note to install a flash drive inside Erasmus for silent operation) and the noise of Kyle puttering around, straightening his tools. He liked things neat.

Eventually, Erasmus found the routine deep in the computer memory of the drum's lock that was supposed to be triggered when the right fingerprint pressed against the scanner. Erasmus went ahead and told that routine to function and the lock popped partially. Then he did the same thing for the routine triggered by the key card, and the lock opened the rest of the way.

"Good job," Kyle told Erasmus. He disconnected the cables and lifted the lid off the drum.

Inside were six long metal cylinders bolted into place inside a bath of liquid nitrogen. Kyle dipped a finger in tentatively at first — he was usually impervious to physical harm, but he'd never tried cold this extreme.

Whew! He blew out a sigh of relief — the liquid nitrogen didn't feel cold at all. Just a little cool. He undid the bolts holding in the first cylinder and pulled it out.

In a dusty corner of the basement was Kyle's biochemical forge, a large, boxy contraption made out of the shell of an old mini refrigerator and the guts of an air-conditioning unit, a discarded breathing apparatus, and two broken microwave ovens. A funnel with a lid led into the forge. Kyle unscrewed the cylinder and poured the contents into the funnel. Once the chemicals hit the guts of the biochemical forge, the forge would start combining and recombining them, creating new compounds, new chemicals, and, eventually, the thing Kyle needed most in the world —

Just then, the kitchen door opened and Kyle heard footfalls on the steps. He looked around for a place to hide the cylinder, but there was nowhere nearby, so he just stood there, the chemicals glug-glugging into the forge as his father came downstairs and beamed at him.

Busted! Kyle froze in mid-glug.

"How — how you doing, slugger?" Dad asked brightly. (Ever since Kyle had used his special brain-wave manipulator to make his father decide not to take the family to the Mighty Mike Day parade a little while ago, Dad had been stuttering on the word *how*. Kyle kept meaning to fix that but then kept forgetting. He was busy.)

"Um, fine, Dad."

"What's this you're doing?" Dad craned his neck to study the cylinder, which was now almost empty.

Kyle took a deep breath. "Well, Dad, I'm stocking the reserves of my biochemical forge so that someday I can breed a custom bacterium that will remove Mighty Mike's superpowers."

Dad stared for a second, then laughed. "Oh, you kids and your crazy ideas from the Internet!" He went back upstairs, chuckling and shaking his head.

It was so convenient to have idiots for parents! Kyle had spent most of his life annoyed by his parents' lack of intelligence, but he had to admit that it made it easier for him to lead a double life.

Kyle finished dumping the rest of the chemicals into the forge, then fiddled with the forge's controls. If his numbers were right — and why wouldn't they be? — he should be able to use this particular chemical combination to generate that special bacterium. And then . . .

"Kyle!" Dad was coming down the steps again.

"What?"

"I forgot why I came down before. Mairi is upstairs waiting for you."

Mairi! Kyle's best friend, Mairi MacTaggert. Of course — he'd forgotten that he had promised to work on a school science project with her this weekend. Sure enough, it was Saturday and Mairi had arrived.

Kyle was so busy — he had to go to school, deal with his parents, plot the destruction of Mighty Mike. . . . Was it any wonder he kept forgetting to fix his parents' brains? (Mom had a twitch that just wouldn't go away — the brain-wave manipulator again.)

He finished up in the basement as quickly as he could and ran upstairs. Mairi was waiting for him in the living room, sitting cross-legged on the floor, her notebook already out and her pen uncapped. Her bright red hair was tied in two pigtails and she smiled when he came in. No matter how annoyed Kyle was, his best friend's smile could always put him in a better mood.

"Hey, Mairi. Sorry. My dad didn't tell me you were here the first time." He rolled his eyes at his father's goof.

"That's okay. He seems a little . . ." Mairi leaned in and whispered, "Have you noticed he stutters a little bit now?"

"No, really?" Kyle asked innocently. On his mental to-do list, he moved *Fix Mom's and Dad's brains* up another level. It still wasn't at the top of the list, but it was getting closer.

"Anyway," he went on, "I have a great idea for the project. We can reproduce the Geiger-Marsden experiment, only in our version, we won't rely on strictly Newtonian analytics. We'll quantify the low-energy alpha-scattering with full quantum mechanical methods, which should yield the same results but will allow us to infer quantum dynamic principles that Rutherford couldn't have imagined."

Mairi stared at him.

"Um . . ." Kyle kicked himself mentally. "Um, what I meant was . . ."

"I was thinking," Mairi began, "that we could test whether or not the color of a crayon determines how long that crayon lasts."

"Sure, sure," Kyle said. "That's what I was thinking. I was kidding about the other stuff."

"Right," Mairi said, but the set of her jaw said that she didn't quite believe it. "Just another one of your pranks, huh?"

"Exactly!" Kyle said a little too enthusiastically, glad for an out. "Exactly."

They spent the next hour or so planning their experiment: which colors they would use (black and white, as well as all the primary colors), what surface (regular white copier paper), and so on. Kyle had to keep reminding himself to be smart, but not *too* smart. He couldn't let Mairi know that he was now the smartest kid on the planet, but he also couldn't be stupid because Mairi knew that Kyle was no dummy.

They were making good progress when a chirping sound interrupted them. Kyle looked around the room. What the heck was —?

Oh. Mairi dug into her pocket and pulled out a tiny cell phone. "Hello?" She listened for a moment and her expression — which had been focused and intent — became light and open and happy. "Oh! Oh! Okay!"

She clicked the phone shut. "Hey, Kyle. I have to, uh, I have to go. Can we finish this another time?"

"Well, yeah, sure. It's not due for a while." He watched her gather up her stuff in a hurry. "Since when do you have a cell phone?"

"Since a week ago, you dummy." She shook her head. "You used to pay attention to everything."

Kyle grimaced. He knew that his campaign to rid the world of Mighty Mike was beginning to take a toll on his so-called "normal" life. He hadn't seen Mairi in more than a week, other than on the bus or at school, for example. And now he'd missed something major like her first cell phone? He had to do a better job balancing his two lives.

"So, uh, what's it for? Emergencies?" He felt stupid for saying that because Mairi looked *very* happy, not the least bit upset, but he couldn't think of another way to find out what was going on.

"Kyle, if you want to know why I have to go, just ask me," she said.

Hmm. Sure, there was always that. "Okay. Why do you have to go?"

Mairi put everything into her backpack and took Kyle's hands in her own. She gazed into his eyes. "Don't get upset, okay? Do you promise?"

"Sure."

"That was my mom. She said Mighty Mike is at my house. I promised him I would hang out with him today."

Kyle snatched his hands back from Mairi's quickly. He didn't want to crush her hands with his incredible strength, and he had a feeling he was going to be making fists soon. He knew that Mighty Mike had hung out at Mairi's house once after "saving" her from a "dirt monster," but now they were making *plans* with each other? "What? But we were —"

"Kyle, you said you wouldn't get upset."

"Yeah, but . . ."

Mairi shook her head. "We were supposed to work on this project a week ago. I promised Mike I'd see him today before you canceled our last meeting."

Oh. Kyle remembered that — a week ago, he'd decided to steal a radioactive element from a government lab three states away. He'd actually failed at that attempt, but his escape had been, of course, spectacular.

"So now you have to go on some kind of date with him, is that it?"

Mairi laughed. "A date? Are you nuts? My dad says I can't go on dates until I'm fourteen. We're just hanging out." She looked at Kyle seriously. "We do that sometimes, you know. He's really lonely."

Lonely. Kyle snorted. "Half the planet is in love with him. How can he be lonely?"

"Because no one else understands what it's like to be him, to have his powers, to be so isolated from everyone else." She thought for a moment. "Well, I guess the Blue Freak *might* understand, but he's no good." And just to make sure Kyle got the point, she shivered.

Kyle bit down on his bottom lip as hard as he dared. It was the best way to keep himself from ranting about how misunderstood the Blue Freak was. He managed to nod in sympathy instead, even though it killed him to pretend that his alter ego was evil.

"Most people just want things from Mike," Mairi went on. "But he knows that he can come over to my house and just hang out and my parents won't ask anything of him."

"Well, that's great," Kyle said, trying to sound sincere. The expression on Mairi's face told him he'd failed, though.

She shrugged into her coat. "You know, you could come over. Hang out with him. He wouldn't mind."

"I better not," Kyle said. "I have some stuff I have to do." Ouch! What a lame excuse! Stuff? He had *stuff* to do?

He walked Mairi to the front door. "You're not planning a new prank, are you?"

Only if you consider wiping Mighty Mike off the map a prank. "Me? Nope!"

"Well, good. You haven't pulled a prank in a while. It's sort of weird to see you so calm, but it's nice, too." She grinned. "Bye! See you later!"

As soon as she was gone, Kyle kicked the fancy wrought-iron table next to the front door, shattering it into pieces. Whoops! Sometimes he forgot his own strength. He quickly gathered up the pieces and compressed them into a big iron ball.

Lonely. The word echoed in his brain over and over, and every time it became more annoying. How could Mighty Mike be lonely when he had screaming, *squee*ing hordes hanging on his every word? *Kyle* was the lonely one. He had once been the most popular kid in all of Bouring, but now the kids at school were all about Mighty Mike, and even Mairi had abandoned him.

Fuming, he stalked downstairs and hid the ball under the staircase. Mighty Mike! Everywhere he turned: Mighty Mike! It was driving him nuts. Bad enough the kid was on this planet at all. Bad enough he showed up to try to stop Kyle's heist. But now he was also hanging out with Kyle's best friend and taking her away from him in the process.

Kyle leaned over the biochemical forge. "Work faster!" he yelled at it. He knew that yelling at it wouldn't make it digest those new chemicals and spit out the results any sooner, but it made him feel a little bit better.

He went back upstairs just as his mother came home from the store. She nudged the door open with her knee, both arms loaded down with packages. Her keys dangled from a finger.

"Kyle, honey? Can you help me with this stuff?"

Kyle took a few packages. He could have carried the entire stack of packages easily, but that would raise suspicions. He pretended they were heavy.

"Thanks, honey," Mom said, and dropped her keys to her left side. They fell straight to the floor and clanged.

Kyle looked around, as if nothing had happened. "Where do you want these packages, Mom?"

His mother stared at her keys where they lay, her face a mixture of disbelief and confusion. "Wasn't . . . wasn't there a *table* here? Before, I mean?"

Kyle looked at her earnestly. "A table? I don't think so."

Mom's brow furrowed. "But I could have *sworn* —"

"I would remember if there had been a table there," he assured her.

"Oh. Well. Okay, then." She smiled. "Just put those things in the kitchen."

Kyle put the packages on the kitchen table and then raced upstairs to his bedroom before his mother could have him do something else. He had more important things to do than menial chores. He flopped down on his bed.

"Hey, Lefty," he said.

Lefty, the big white New Zealand rabbit who lived in a cage in Kyle's room, tilted his head at Kyle, regarding him with one pink-red eye. When Kyle was younger, he used to imagine that Lefty could understand him, but he knew that wasn't true. Lefty's head was no bigger than a baseball — there wasn't a lot of room for a brain in there, and most of that limited brainpower was focused on remembering to poop in the litter box.

Still, Kyle loved Lefty. No matter what happened, Lefty always licked Kyle's hand and chinned him. (There was no higher praise from a rabbit than to be chinned by one.) Lefty never talked back or laughed at Kyle, and he never demanded anything more complicated than a chunk of dried papaya or a fruit-flavored yogurt drop.

"We're gonna watch TV, Lefty," Kyle declared, hefting the rabbit out of the cage and plopping him on the bed. He reached for his remote and turned on his two TVs.

Yes, two TVs. Kyle hated TV — the shows were dumb and he despised the slack-jawed expressions of idiocy that people wore while watching it — but lately he had become obsessed with watching footage of himself on the news. For the first few days, he'd just watched on his laptop, but the screen was too small, the connection too slow, the video jerky and pixelated.

So he'd scavenged at a local recycling plant one night and dug up two truly awesome flat screens. Plasma technology, fifty-five inches. Great stuff. They were a little scuffed and had burned-out power supplies, but Kyle was able to patch them up easily. Then he used a couple of discarded TiVos and voilà! He had his own media recording studio, with magnificent playback.

The whole thing had to be hidden in his closet, lest his parents ask him where the TVs had come from.

He locked his bedroom door as the TVs roared to life. Fortunately, he had calculated — correctly, as it turned out — that Channels Five and Thirteen would be the most likely local stations to get news crews to Axis, so he'd set the TiVos to record those two channels.

"This should be fun," he told Lefty. Lefty nuzzled Kyle's arm until Kyle started petting him, then settled in next to Kyle.

The footage at the chemical factory was better and more impressive than he could have dreamed. With his enhanced intellect, Kyle had no problem watching two TVs at once. He was slightly annoyed by the crawl along the bottom of Channel Five's screen, which said, "SUPERVILLAIN ATTACKS CHEMICAL PLANT." Channel Thirteen was a little more diplomatic: "MASKED FIGURE STEALS RARE CHEMICALS." Which was true, if simpleminded.

Still, none of that mattered when he focused on the action. He looked amazing floating up there as the cameras tried to track him. He never got tired of watching himself, of seeing something that looked like a movie special effect, but that he knew was real . . . and was *him*.

He heard himself laugh over his built-in PA and watched the cops and the Army guys fire off their fusillade of weapons. But on-screen, he dodged them all. The moment when he knocked aside a rocket was amazing. Channel Five played it a couple of times in slo-mo, which Kyle appreciated. It was important for people to see how cool he was.

But that paled in comparison to watching himself in action against Mighty Mike. Kyle was enthralled, staring bug-eyed at the TVs as his on-screen self effortlessly dodged Mighty Mike and basically made the kid look like the chump he truly was. To top it all off, the laser-chaff grenade was *totally* impressive in high-def. Kyle actually gasped out loud and said to Lefty, "Did you see that? That's mine! I did that!" and rewound it on both screens to watch from two angles as the chaff filled the air. As a bonus, he got to watch again as Mighty Mike flew right into the chaff and got blinded. Kyle cackled. Truly, the simple things made life worth living.

Kyle watched what had happened after he left: The Air Force jets arrived moments later and their wakes blew away most of the laser-chaff. Mighty Mike shook his head to clear his vision, wobbling in the air as if drunk, then took off in the completely wrong direction. The news cameras showed cops and soldiers running here and there, scattering, then coming back together. It was chaos, confusion. No one had the slightest hope of figuring out where Kyle had gone. Excellent.

Afterward, Kyle watched as Mike gave a brief, impromptu interview to the reporter from Channel Five. "The Blue Freak can't avoid me forever," he said, gazing earnestly into the camera. "Eventually, I'll hammer him down." Mike's brain damage was legendary. Kyle couldn't keep from guffawing every time Mike misspoke.

"Of course by that you mean you'll nail him?" the reporter asked.

"Don't help him!" Kyle yelled at the TV. "Let everyone see what an idiot he is!"

Mike smiled and thought for a moment. Kyle imagined he could see tiny gears turning in the alien brat's minuscule alien excuse for a brain.

"That's exactly what I meant. Thank you."

"Of course."

"That's not what he meant," Kyle mumbled. Everyone covered for Mighty Mike. Life just wasn't fair.

CHAPTER
THREE

That night, as Kyle slept and the biochemical forge churned to itself in the basement, as Erasmus dozed in an electronic version of sleep and Lefty pawed at his litter and chewed on blocks of wood (rabbits are normally crepuscular, not nocturnal, but Lefty was an insomniac bunny), the masked figure from the Axis parking lot sneaked through the woods behind the Camden house.

The lanky, cloaked figure stole through the dark, the eyeholes of his mask now a sickly green . . . the green glow of night vision.

He picked his way along carefully, a small handheld gadget held out before him. The gadget beeped slowly, methodically.

Occasionally, the figure would stop and crouch down, poking at the dirt with one gloved finger or pulling up a weed to scrutinize it with those steadily glowing green eyes.

The quiet, steady beep continued as he made his way deeper into the woods.

Then, suddenly, the pace of the beeps increased.

The figure paused. He swung the gadget to the left.

The beeps slowed down.

To the right.

The beeps speeded up.

Yes!

He turned right and walked faster, ducking under branches and gathering his cloak tight around himself to avoid being caught in the brambles. The beeps came faster . . .

. . . and faster . . .

. . . and faster!

Finally, the figure stopped, double-checked his gadget, and knelt down again. He scanned the ground for a moment, then brushed away some dead leaves and dug out a handful of soft dirt.

There, in the ground near a large, gnarled tree, was a hatch. It was locked with a very complicated electronic lock — it had a keypad and a number screen that went up to twelve numbers. That meant there were $10^1 + 10^2 + 10^3 \ldots 10^{12}$ possible combinations: 1,111,111,111,110 in total. Well over one trillion.

The masked figure made a single, short noise under his mask. It might have been a grunt. It might have been a chuckle. He fiddled with the lock for a moment and popped it open, then lifted the hatch.

Underneath was a small, boxy space. And inside . . .

The costume of the Blue Freak!

from the top secret journal of
Kyle Camden (deciphered):

The rest of the world refers to the creature that attacked Mairi as "the dirt monster," an appellation that betrays a deadly lack of imagination. It wasn't a "dirt monster." It was an Animated Soil Entity — ASE. I pronounce it "ace." That's a much better name, and more accurate, too.

Anyway, a few days after the incident with the ASE, the FBI put me on the Most Wanted list. At number one.

I'm always happy to be the best at something, but this wasn't terribly convenient. Basically, every single FBI agent and cop in the world is on the lookout for me now. I am (or, rather, the "Blue Freak" is) considered a "national security risk." The technical term they use is (get this): "unauthorized supra-endowed civilian actor."

This means that I have powers and I don't let anyone boss me around.

I am wanted for the following crimes, none of which I committed:

- **Destruction of public property, multiple counts** (Well, okay, I did that one, but it was an accident.)
- **Destruction of private property, multiple counts** (All right, they got me there, too, but again — it was an accident. My Pants Laser malfunctioned

when I was trying to vaporize Mighty Mike's pants. If he hadn't flown up and grabbed the Pants Laser, I could have disabled it without causing further harm to anyone. How is this my fault?)

- **Assault** *(No way! I just tried to vaporize pants! How is that assault? I'm the one who was assaulted — Mighty Mike punched me! In public. Not cool.)*

- **Assault with a deadly weapon, two counts** *(One for the Pants Laser — which wasn't supposed to be deadly! — and one for the ASE, which I had nothing to do with!)*

- **Unlicensed use of extranormal powers** *(This is a crime? Really?)*

In any event, I am clearly misunderstood by The Powers That Be, which only serves to reinforce my long-held conviction that The Powers That Be are, in fact, mentally deficient subhuman drone-brains. These are the kind of people who need help figuring out how to tie their shoes in the morning. They would probably forget to breathe if you didn't remind them. I would call them morons, but that would be insulting to morons.

So.

It's one thing to have a basement full of gadgets, chemicals, and other assorted detritus of my campaign to destroy Mighty Mike. It's quite another thing to have the costume of the FBI's Most Wanted. My experiments are so sophisticated that they would look like incomprehensible junk to most people, but even the stupidest cop would know the "Blue Freak's" outfit on sight.

This is why I store my costume off-site, hidden out in the woods. For safety and plausible deniability. Truly I am a genius.

CHAPTER
FOUR

"Kyle!" The voice yanked Kyle from sleep, pulling him from what might have been the greatest dream in the history of dreams. In the dream, he had just gotten Mighty Mike in a headlock on national television. As an entire brigade of soldiers threatened to open fire on him if he didn't let the "hero" go, Kyle paused for dramatic effect and then — in one smooth motion — ripped off the special mask Mighty Mike had been wearing as a human face, revealing a greenish-blue, scaly alien face underneath. Kyle was reasonably certain that Mighty Mike did not, in fact, have scaly skin hidden under a mask, but it was a great dream, so he wasn't about to question it. In the dream, he held the mask up and shouted, "Mighty Mike is *not* our friend!"

"Kyle!" the voice called again. Kyle tried to ignore it and sink back into the dream. The dream was great. The dream was awesome. Real life, not so much.

"Kyle! Please wake up!"

Groaning, Kyle fumbled at his nightstand for Erasmus,

who was yelling at him and flashing his screen to light up the room. "What is it, Erasmus? I need my sleep."

"Someone is tampering with the costume bunker!"

Kyle bolted upright in bed. He had connected the locking mechanism on his costume's hiding place to Erasmus wirelessly, just in case. He couldn't imagine how someone could possibly crack his impossible-to-crack electronic lock, but still . . .

He quickly threw on a pair of black pants and a black sweatshirt. After a second, he decided to pull on a black ski mask, too. It was sort of cliché, but he had to hide his face. The odds were that some animal had stumbled upon the bunker and somehow activated the alarm, but he couldn't take any chances. His freedom, his privacy, his very identity were all at stake.

He opened the window. "Hold down the fort, Lefty," he said. Lefty, thinking he was getting a treat, bounded over to the side of the cage nearest to the window and started pulling on the wire with his teeth.

Kyle flew out the window as fast as he dared to go. Even with the light from a full moon, anyone who happened to be looking in that direction at that exact moment *might* see a blur in the night sky, but that was it.

He was moving so fast that it only took seconds to get to the costume bunker, weaving through the denuded tree branches, diving low to the carpet of fallen leaves on the ground. Just before he arrived at the bunker, he picked out a figure standing near the tree, almost blending in with the shadows cast by the moonlight.

And the figure was holding Kyle's costume!

Kyle landed a few feet away from the interloper and took him in. He was tall and lanky, draped in a dark green cloak. His hands — the left one held the costume up in the air like a trophy — wore heavy leather gauntlets that matched his buckled boots. But most impressive was the mask.

It was jet-black, shaped like two half ovals that had been joined off-center, such that one protruded at the top and the other at the bottom. An inlaid ivory tear wept down one cheek. Both eyes glowed green.

"Greetings," the figure said. He chuckled, the sound low and echoing in the mask.

Kyle darted toward him, a blur of speed, reaching out for his costume. Before his fingers could touch it, though, he saw and heard a loud, hot electrical crackle that jerked his arm so powerfully that he felt as if it would come right out of his shoulder socket. At the very same instant, the power of that shock spun him around and threw him back ten feet to smack against a tree.

What . . . ? What had just happened . . . ?

Kyle snarled and gathered his wits for another try. But the figure held up his other hand in a warning gesture.

"Do not attempt to lay hands on the Mad Mask

again! This force field is strong enough to deflect any attack . . . but you are not strong enough to survive its full power!"

Kyle gritted his teeth together. He wasn't sure he believed "the Mad Mask," but that shock had been the only thing to hurt him other than Mighty Mike and the ASE since he'd gained his powers. Maybe this guy wasn't full of baloney. Maybe his force field really was that powerful.

"What do you want?" he demanded. "Why do you have my costume?"

"*Your* costume. Then you are, in fact, the Blue Freak." The Mad Mask said nothing for a moment. "Aren't you a little short for a supervillain?"

"Turn off that force field and you'll see that size doesn't matter," Kyle retorted.

The Mad Mask laughed, a throaty, terrifying sound. "Well met, Blue Freak. Or do you prefer to be called the Azure Avenger? Oh, yes," he said as Kyle's jaw dropped under the ski mask, "the Mad Mask's audio enhancer technology detected your conversation while you flew above Axis. Who is your partner? Who is 'Erasmus'?"

So, the Mad Mask had heard Kyle's conversation with Erasmus. "Maybe I'll tell you that," Kyle said, "and maybe I won't. First I want to know why you're here and what you want." While he seethed outwardly, inside

Kyle was relieved that the Mad Mask obviously didn't know his real identity. He didn't need that kind of information getting out there.

"Your posture is aggressive and worrisome, Azure Avenger. Relax. There is no need to fear the Mad Mask. The Mad Mask means you no harm." As if to prove it, he held out the costume. Kyle crept closer, wary of the force field, and reached out, half expecting another shock. When no shock came, he snatched his costume away from the Mad Mask.

"Why did you take my costume? How did you break into my costume bunker?"

The Mad Mask laughed again. "The Mad Mask sought you, not your costume. Fortunately — and predictably — one led to the other. As to your 'bunker' . . . Your electronic lock may as well have been a bungee cord to the technological genius of the Mad Mask!"

"But how did you even find it in the first place?"

"Examine your cape."

Kyle pawed at the cape until his finger touched a small, hard nodule that shouldn't have been there. He groaned.

"You fired some kind of tracking beacon at me."

The Mad Mask bowed with a flourish.

Kyle made a mental note to install a bug detector in Erasmus so that this couldn't happen again. He moved that particular to-do item to the very top of the list.

"Okay, so you tracked me down and you got what you wanted. You found me. I'm assuming you're not working for the FBI or the government because I would already be surrounded by cops."

"The government!" The Mad Mask spat out the words with such a fury that Kyle wondered how gross the inside of that mask looked right now. "Dunderheads! Mewling idiot-children!"

Kyle decided that maybe the Mad Mask wasn't all bad.

"Incompetent, brainless dullards!" the Mad Mask went on. "The Mad Mask recognizes no government, no authority higher than his own inimitable genius!"

Kyle realized that the guy still hadn't bothered to explain what he was doing here.

"The Mad Mask has his own agenda," he continued. "The Mad Mask hails from nearby, yet the Mad Mask's genius is too large for this region, for Bouring, for the state, the country, indeed the *world*! And so, the Mad Mask has made ready to strike out at the world at large and make his mark upon the planet!"

Here the Mad Mask paused, as if expecting Kyle to say or do something. Kyle thought quickly and said, "Um, that's quite an impressive mask you've got there." It was true — Kyle sort of had mask-envy. His own mask was just an old blanket that he had cut and sewed into a new shape. It itched.

The Mad Mask cleared his throat somewhere in that big cloak. "Oh. Yes. The mask. Thank you. I, uh, made it in shop class."

Shop class?

"Er, I mean . . ." he said, his voice rising in volume and deepening, "the Mad Mask fashioned and assembled it over many hard and laborious hours in shop class!

"But let us not speak of such things now!" The Mad Mask gestured with both hands and the cloak rippled and waved very impressively. "The Mad Mask has come here with an offer for you, Azure Avenger."

"What kind of an offer?" Kyle had to admit that it sounded pretty cool to hear someone else — finally! — call him the Azure Avenger.

"The Mad Mask is constructing . . . Ultitron!" He shouted the last word and then waited, panting slightly, as if Kyle was supposed to know what he was talking about.

"Uh, what's Ultitron?" Kyle asked after a long silence.

"What is Ultitron? What is Ultitron?" The Mad Mask threw his hands up in the air as if to say, *Do you see what I have to deal with?* "Ultitron is only the ultimate engine of devastation and destruction. That's all. It's only an artificially intelligent humanoid techno-configuration that outpaces all current and next-generation and *next*-next-generation cybernetics technology on the planet!"

"Right. So it's a robot."

The Mad Mask punched a tree. Kyle couldn't believe it.

"A robot? Would you call the Sistine Chapel a church? Would you call the Sphinx a statue? Would you call —"

"Okay, okay, I hear you. It's *the* robot." Kyle didn't want to listen to any more ranting. He wanted to get to the point, so: "Get to the point," he said.

"Work on Ultitron continues apace. However, the Mad Mask has come to realize that — despite his inimitable genius and impeccable design skills — the process could be accelerated with the addition of a similar, though inferior, intellect. Consequently, the Mad Mask invites you to act as *sous chef* to his masterpiece!"

Kyle brushed aside the insult. "So you need my help to finish your robot, is what you're saying."

The Mad Mask bristled. "The Mad Mask has said and will say no such thing! The Mad Mask has graciously and magnanimously decided to extend to you the honor of assisting in the completion of the mighty Ultitron! In exchange for your time and efforts, the Mad Mask will set Ultitron upon your enemy."

Kyle's eyes widened. Had he heard that correctly? All he had to do was help this guy finish his robot . . . and then they would send the robot after Mighty Mike?

He thought about that powerful force field, so strong that it had hurt even him. If it could hurt Kyle, then wasn't there a chance that it could hurt Mighty Mike, too? After all, Mike's powers were from the same power source as Kyle's — the plasma storm.

And then there was the fact that the Mad Mask had cracked Kyle's electronic lock, which had over a trillion possible combinations. That should have been impossible.

Anyone with that kind of smarts . . . with that kind of powerful technology . . .

A slow expression of absolute joy spread over Kyle's face under his ski mask as he imagined Mighty Mike getting the stuffing pounded out of him by this "Ultitron" thing. Preferably while Mairi watched and realized her hero wasn't all he was cracked up to be.

"You've got a deal," Kyle said. "We'll finish Ultitron together and then I get to use it to kick Mighty Mike off the planet."

The Mad Mask approached Kyle. With that mask in place, Kyle couldn't see even the slightest hint of a facial expression. He had no idea what the Mad Mask was thinking.

And then the Mad Mask extended one gloved hand. "We have an accord, then!"

As they shook on it, the Mad Mask's voice suddenly dropped and became a little shaky. "So, uh, how old are you, anyway?"

"Twelve," Kyle told him.

"Twelve!" The voice was back to full boom. "The Mad Mask is fourteen! Thus, the Mad Mask shall be in charge!"

"Well, that's fine. It's your robot, after all."

"It is, indeed, the Mad Mask's robot!"

They stood there for a moment, hands still clasped, saying nothing.

"So, uh, what do we do now?" Kyle asked.

"The Mad Mask will prepare his facilities for you! We will meet at noon on the morrow . . . there!" He pointed with his free hand to the Bouring Lighthouse, barely visible in the distance through the tree branches.

"Okay, fine." Kyle extricated himself from the Mad Mask's grasp. "Great. I'll see you there tomorrow."

"On the morrow!" the Mad Mask bellowed.

"Right. Got it."

More silence. More staring at each other.

Kyle realized that the Mad Mask was waiting for him to leave. *He can't fly! And he doesn't want me to watch him walk away.*

"See you tomorrow," Kyle said, and launched himself skyward. He stopped just before clearing the treetops and entering the open air. Still concealed, he checked his costume thoroughly. There was only the one bug. He held it between his thumb and forefinger for a moment, admiring its compact design.

Then he rotated in midair, looking for the Mad Mask. He would follow from the sky, tracking the Mad Mask back to wherever he'd come from. No one could just barge in on Kyle's life like this without . . .

But the Mad Mask was nowhere to be seen. He was gone in the few moments Kyle had been distracted by the bug.

Kyle grunted in disappointment, then crushed the bug into powder and let the particles drift away on the breeze.

When he flew back in through the window, both Erasmus and Lefty went berserk. Lefty was the easier of the two to handle — Kyle stroked the rabbit's head, scratched behind his ears, and then dropped a yogurt treat into the cage.

"What happened?" Erasmus asked. If the AI had needed to breathe, Kyle would have said Erasmus sounded breathless.

"It was . . . strange," Kyle said. He told Erasmus what had happened and what he'd agreed to do.

"I never thought I'd live to see the day when Kyle Camden would work *for* somebody," Erasmus said with a note of snobbery.

"First of all, you're not really alive. Second of all, you can't see anything because you don't have eyes."

"Don't try to distract me with petty details."

Kyle closed his window, got back into his pajamas, and lay down in bed. "I don't know, Erasmus. You weren't there. You didn't see what he was capable of. He cracked the electronic lock. That should have taken a couple thousand years."

"So he got lucky."

"Hmm. Maybe you're right. But if that's the case . . . Heck, Erasmus — I think I could stand to get a little bit of that kind of luck. Don't you?"

And to that, Erasmus had nothing to say.

from the top secret journal of
Kyle Camden (deciphered):

I'm so excited I can't sleep. And I'm having a little trouble holding the pen to write this, too!

For the first time since I gained my powers, I have an ally. An actual ally!

(Erasmus doesn't count because I built and programmed him. He has no choice — he has to work with me.)

I know it's only been a few weeks since Mighty Mike was revealed to the world, but it's felt like years, with everyone praising him and celebrating him and — ugh — loving him. There are even some kids at school who have started wearing capes again, and one of Mom's idiotic fashion shows on TV says that "the summer collection" (whatever that is) will probably "feature lots of draped fabric." In other words — capes!

(And, yes, I realize that the Azure Avenger wears a cape. That's to dissuade people from associating me with the Azure Avenger. Since I would never be caught dead wearing a cape, I couldn't possibly be the Azure Avenger. See?)

Now, out of nowhere, comes the Mad Mask.

I realize he has an . . . interesting way of talking, but . . .

(Oh, who am I kidding? He's annoying as heck when he talks!)

But the thing is, he's obviously a genius. To be able to plant a tracking device on me . . . To be able to open the electronic lock . . . Yes, he has his quirks, but he's finally someone I can work with.

More important than that, though . . . He's someone who believes in me.

He offered up his "Ultitron" (I can't wait to see this thing!) without hesitation, without worry. He understands that Mighty Mike needs to be booted off the planet, and if Ultitron's boots are big enough to do it, then great! I can't afford to be picky in my choice of allies. The Mad Mask wants to help me achieve my dream, and all I need to do is help him achieve his dream.

Sounds good to me.

(added later)

I just realized, though: What is *the Mad Mask's dream?*
I'll have to ask him.

And in the meantime, I've got Erasmus thinking
about ways to crack that force field. It's one thing to
trust an ally. It's another thing to trust an ally who can
hurt you.

CHAPTER
FIVE

Kyle dragged himself out of bed Sunday morning, barely able to pry his eyes open. He had amazing powers, true, but he still needed to sleep, and last night's shenanigans with the Mad Mask had zapped his sleep time down to almost nil.

In the kitchen, his parents were bustling about as usual, blabbering to each other while the kitchen TV showed an extended series of film clips of Mighty Mike: Mike hauling a damaged sub out of the ocean. Mike putting out a forest fire. Mike petting a dog. In each clip, Kyle saw mistakes Mike made — a potential radiation leak left unsealed on the sub, embers blowing in the breeze at the forest fire. Even the dog looked a little annoyed that Mike was just rubbing his one ear over and over again.

Mike did these huge good deeds and everyone was happy, but no one ever noticed that a lot of times he also made mistakes. Or if they did notice, they were so impressed with him anyway that they didn't care. That was wrong. And stupid. And wrong again. It annoyed Kyle, even when he wasn't tired.

He slumped into a chair at the table and stared at Dad's ginormous coffee cup. It was as big as a soup bowl and had SUPERCHARGED! written on it in big block letters.

"Can I have some coffee?" Kyle asked.

His parents stopped chattering to each other. Mom, standing by the toaster, blinked slowly, as if she couldn't believe what she was seeing. Which was moronic because Kyle had *said* something. She should have been not believing her *ears*, not her eyes.

"Coffee's for grown-ups," Mom chirped.

"Yeah, slugger," Dad agreed, hoisting his cup and wincing a bit at the weight. "Kids don't need a pick-me-up." He guzzled.

"I didn't sleep well," Kyle said. "I want to wake up."

"You're only eleven . . ." Dad started.

"I'm twelve," Kyle said.

"Really?" Dad looked at Mom as if she could somehow change the flow of time. Mom shrugged. "How — how long has *that* been going on?"

"Since my birthday, pretty much."

"Huh!"

Saying — or, rather, grunting — "Huh!" like that was Kyle's dad's most common utterance. It had, as best Kyle could tell, roughly three dozen different meanings (at last count), running the gamut from "That's fine" to "Leave me alone" to "Why, that is a most interesting and compelling fact, the likes of which I had previously been unaware." In this specific instance, Kyle translated "Huh!" as meaning, "Wow, time sure flies when you're busy watching TV and eating pizza bagels."

"I guess it won't hurt to let him try a little," Mom said. "As long as it doesn't become a regular thing."

She poured a bit of coffee into a mug that was significantly smaller than Dad's and offered it to him. Kyle inhaled the rich, dark aroma. He loved the smell of coffee and had often fantasized about this adult ritual.

He grinned as he saluted his parents with the mug. "Thanks, guys." He took a big gulp of the stuff.

And spat it right back out into the mug!

Gross!

Mom laughed. Dad shook his head and turned to his newspaper.

Oh, disgusting! It was like drinking a cup of hot bilge. The stuff was bitter and strong. How could something that smelled so wonderful taste so awful? He added yet another item to his mental to-do list: *Fix the flavor of coffee.* Why hadn't someone else handled this yet? People had been drinking coffee for over five hundred years (according to Wikipedia, which he had memorized awhile back), but no one noticed until Kyle took his first sip that it tasted terrible?

It was as though every day, in some small way, the universe wanted to remind Kyle that he was an intellectual titan living in a world of mental microbes.

"How can you drink this stuff?" Kyle asked, spitting again into his mug. Mom brought him a glass of juice and Kyle guzzled it in gratitude.

"It's an acquired taste," Mom admitted.

"Not for me!" Kyle said.

After a quick breakfast, he went into the living room, where the materials for his project with Mairi were stacked on the coffee table. Seeing the pile depressed Kyle for two reasons. First of all, it was a ridiculous experiment — he could easily figure out in his head if crayon color affected how long a crayon lasted. He didn't need a fancy experiment to deduce wax retention based on pigmentation. Second of all, it reminded him that his best friend was, slowly, slipping away.

At first, Kyle had thought that it would be fun to live a double life. His activities as the Azure Avenger, the existence of Erasmus . . . These were his deepest secrets, the things that no one knew about him. He knew from his history of pulling pranks that having a secret was fun.

But this secret was time-consuming and exhausting. For the past several weeks, he'd been so focused on working to destroy Mighty Mike that he had neglected his "real life" as Kyle Camden. There was actually a period of three days in a row where he hadn't spoken to Mairi at all. Unheard of!

Just then, the doorbell rang, cutting off Kyle's moping. He ran to the door and smiled a huge, broad smile when he saw Mairi standing there. It was only fall, but it was a supercold fall, so Mairi looked like she was ready for winter, bundled up in her white puffy coat, her red hair a flaming ring around her face.

"Hey, Kyle!"

It was like the universe decided to cut him a break.

"I figured I'd come over and we could keep working on the science project. Is now a good time?"

"Sure," Kyle said, stepping aside to let her in. "It's . . ."

He broke off as something caught his eye outside. Off in the distance, the Bouring Lighthouse rose stark and alone on the horizon, the highest point in or around Bouring.

"On the morrow . . ."

Kyle checked the time. It was almost noon.

"Kyle?" Mairi was inside now, staring at him as he stood at the open door. "Are you coming in, too?"

"Yeah, yeah, I, uh . . ." His mind whirled, looking for some excuse that could get rid of Mairi, but he couldn't think of anything.

"I forgot — I have something I have to do today," he blurted out. "Right now," he added.

"What? Can I help?"

Kyle briefly imagined himself and the Mad Mask poring over the innards of Ultitron, with Mairi in the background, offering to bring over a wrench or a soldering iron.

"Um, no. I have to do it alone."

Mairi planted her fists on her hips, a stance Kyle knew all too well. "What's so important that you have to go running off on a Sunday? Is it some silly prank?"

A prank! Of course! He couldn't actually admit to it, but . . .

"I . . . don't know what you're talking about," Kyle said in a tone of voice that said he knew *exactly* what she was talking about, but just didn't want to cop to it.

Mairi threw her hands up in the air and marched out the door. "I can't believe you would rather waste your time on a *prank* than work on our project together!"

"Hey!" Kyle shouted after her before he could stop himself. "*You're* the one who had to leave yesterday to go hang out with Mighty Mike!"

She spun around and glared at him. "I explained that."

"We could have finished the whole thing then, but you had to go play with your boyfriend!"

Mairi stamped an angry foot. "I was ready to work on it before. *You're* the one who bailed. And get it straight — he's *not* my boyfriend!" And she turned and stormed off before he could say anything else.

Kyle raced up the stairs. He paused at the hallway window and looked out — he could see Mairi going up the street to her house, her pace quickened by her anger. He hated making Mairi angry at him. It was pretty much the worst thing he'd ever done in his life, and now it seemed like he was doing it all the time. But he had no choice. He couldn't tell her the truth. For one thing, Mairi unfortunately believed the popular lie that the "Blue Freak" was some kind of villain. And for another thing, it wouldn't be right to burden her with the knowledge that Mighty Mike was an alien and that Kyle was the only person alive who could expose and destroy him. If Mike found out Mairi knew, who knew what he might do to her?

No, Kyle had to keep his secrets, no matter what it meant to his best friend.

Someday soon, after he and the Mad Mask finished Ultitron, he would be done with Mighty Mike. And then he and Mairi could go back to being friends, the way it was supposed to be.

It was too risky to fly in broad daylight, so Kyle walked to the lighthouse, his costume stuffed into his backpack, Erasmus in his pocket and talking through his new wireless earbuds. To anyone out on this crisp fall day, it would just look like he was out for a hike.

"Are you sure about this?" Erasmus asked. "Just walking right up to this guy? Can you really trust him?"

"What are you, my mother?" Kyle retorted. "Besides, I'm pretty much indestructible."

"You said that force field hurt you last night."

"Yeah, but that's because I attacked him. As long as I keep my hands off him, I'll be fine."

"If he can make a force field that can hurt you, what if he can make a weapon that can —"

"Get off my back!" Kyle exploded. A man walking on the other side of the street looked over at him curiously. Kyle grinned and waved to assure him everything was fine, then lowered his voice. "Look, he can't fly, okay? Worst case scenario, I'll just zoom away."

"I'll feel more secure when we figure out how to crack that force field," Erasmus grumbled. "Just be careful around him. Remember the words of my namesake: 'A good portion of speaking will consist in knowing how to lie.'"

"Got it," Kyle said as they reached the lighthouse.

The Bouring Lighthouse reached up to the sky and even higher, it seemed. Kyle had flown around it one night and it didn't seem large or imposing from up in the sky. Down here, though, it seemed as massive as it had when he'd first seen it as a young child.

He had to be careful not to be seen by Mrs. MacTaggert while he was here. Mairi's mom was the keeper of the

Bouring Lighthouse and curator of the Lighthouse Museum. No one knew why there was a lighthouse at the edge of Bouring, because the town was landlocked. There was no need for a lighthouse — no lakes or rivers. There wasn't even a good-size stream anywhere nearby.

Kyle skirted the entrance to the lighthouse and went around back. He had spent many hours playing around the lighthouse with Mairi; he knew all of the secret hiding places. He found an old drainage ditch near a sewer outlet and quickly changed into his Azure Avenger costume, tucking Erasmus into a pouch on his belt.

"Well, here we go," he said. He hid his backpack in some brush and slowly crept around the back of the lighthouse.

His heart thrummed wildly, racing with excitement. Kyle had never felt so close to his ultimate goal, to the destruction of Mighty Mike!

He wondered: What would his life be like once Mighty Mike was no longer a part of it? Things couldn't go back to the way they'd been before. After all, Kyle had special powers now, to say nothing of his vastly expanded intellect. He couldn't just . . . retire, could he? Go back to being plain old Kyle Camden, playing pranks like always?

He couldn't imagine it. He would probably still play pranks — pranks were important, after all — but to pretend to be normal? Still? No. He couldn't do it.

Once Mighty Mike's true nature was revealed and the alien was gone for good, Kyle could reveal his true self to the world. Mairi would be upset at his deception, but she would understand that Mike's threat forced his hand. So would everyone else. Maybe he could be the Azure Avenger full time. . . . His parents would finally be so proud of him. . . .

"Kyle." Erasmus's voice interrupted his pleasant fantasy. "It's noon exactly."

Kyle looked around. Where was the Mad Mask?

CHAPTER
SIX

Deep in his hidden lair, the Mad Mask toiled away, feverishly typing on a keyboard with one hand while drawing on an electronic slate with the other. (The Mad Mask was not born ambidextrous, but learning how to do a different task with each hand was simplicity itself to the likes of the Mad Mask!) His ebony mask sat on the workbench next to him, watching as he slaved away.

"Soon," he cackled to himself. "Soon! The Mad Mask's plans are nearly complete! Soon, Ultitron! Soon, you will range over the world, executing your diabolical mission with the perfection only the Mad Mask can envision and only you can perform!"

He talked out loud because it made his thoughts more important, to have them out in the air as opposed to merely confined to the Mad Mask's own head.

"With the help of the Azure Avenger, Ultitron will revenge myself on the world! And once the Azure Avenger has performed his duties . . . he will no longer be of any use to the Mad Mask. . . ."

Under the voluminous sleeve of his cloak, a beeping sound interrupted his soliloquy. It was the alarm on his digital watch.

"Ah! The Mad Mask must go! It is time to bring my new . . . associate up to speed on the design of the magnificent Ultitron! Fortunately, with the help of this matter transmitter" — he picked up a small box from a shelf — "the Mad Mask will be instantly teleported to the Bouring Lighthouse!"

With that, the Mad Mask gathered his electronic slate and slipped his mask into place. He threw back his head and laughed, long and loud.

The matter transmitter flashed and then the lair was empty, with only the echo of the Mad Mask's crazed laughter remaining to fill it.

CHAPTER
SEVEN

A sudden burst of light caught Kyle off guard, flaring, then dimming. Kyle's glare-filters had once again come in handy, automatically sliding into place at the first sign of excessive brightness. Sometimes Kyle's genius impressed even him.

"The Mad Mask appreciates punctuality! Your timeliness is noted!" crowed the Mad Mask as the light vanished.

Kyle's jaw dropped. He teleported! The Mad Mask actually *teleported*! That should be impossible. Kyle had spent a lot of time thinking about a teleportation device. The energy requirements were off the charts, and the massive displacement of air at the arrival point — to say nothing of the sudden vacuum at the point of departure — were flaws he hadn't been able to overcome.

And yet . . . Here was the Mad Mask. Instantly.

"How — how did you do that?" Kyle asked, aware that he had just stuttered like his father.

The Mad Mask waved off the question as though it were beneath him. Then, as if making sure Kyle got the point, he said, "Such questions are beneath the Mad Mask!"

Kyle bristled. He was impressed, yeah, but he wasn't about to let the Mad Mask treat him like some kind of flunky. "If we're going to be partners, you need to trust me," he said. "I'm going to learn your technology anyway."

The Mad Mask considered. He actually stroked the underside of his mask between a thumb and forefinger, as if stroking a beard. Kyle realized now the *real* reason why the Mad Mask had waited for Kyle to fly away last night — he didn't want Kyle to see him teleporting. Maybe now, though, he was beginning to trust Kyle.

"You speak truthfully," the Mad Mask conceded. "In time, the Mad Mask will teach you the secrets of his technology. For now, we will begin with the magnificent Ultitron. Then, when you have learned enough, we will explore the miracles of teleportation! Together! The Azure Avenger and the Mad Mask!"

This last was shouted so loudly that Kyle looked around to make sure no one had overheard.

"Okay, that sounds fair," he agreed, after making sure they were still alone.

The Mad Mask tilted his head, gazing up at the lighthouse as it towered over them. "Beautiful . . ." he murmured, almost inaudible through the mask. "Quite . . . beautiful . . ."

"Can we get started?" Kyle asked. There would be plenty of time to admire the architecture later.

The Mad Mask produced an electronic slate from under his cloak and held it out to Kyle. "On this slate, you will find the schematics and blueprints for the splendid Ultitron, along with the Mad Mask's design notes!"

Kyle hesitated, looking at the slate and the hand that held it, remembering the power of the force field.

"Fear not!" the Mad Mask said. "The Mad Mask's force field detects threats, not casual touches. You will not be harmed!"

Kyle took the slate. "Could you stop referring to yourself in the third person? It's sort of confusing. And I think all the shouting is giving me a headache."

The other shrugged. "The Mad Mask shall endeavor to lower his voice and to avoid the third person!"

Kyle sighed and flipped on the slate. His eyes bugged out behind his mask. The plans were the craziest, most complicated things he'd ever seen . . . and this was coming from the guy currently transforming an old motorbike into a time machine. He studied them for a moment, trying to get his bearings, but nothing seemed to make sense. Needless to say, Kyle wasn't used to being in this position.

"This is . . . interesting," he said, stalling. He flicked through the screens on the slate, schematics whirring by, looking for something he could recognize, anything at all, just something to get a grip on . . .

Finally he stopped. This looked familiar. It was . . . a foot.

A gigantic foot.

Kyle scrutinized it for a moment. This couldn't be . . .

"Is this to scale?" he asked, bringing the slate closer to his eyes. At the same time, that brought it within Erasmus's Wi-Fi range. Now Erasmus could read the slate, too.

"This is . . . crazy . . ." Erasmus whispered in Kyle's ear, sounding — for the first time ever — impressed.

"All images are to scale," the Mad Mask said, like a commercial.

"But this foot is enormous!" Kyle said. "If the scale is right, then the whole robot will be something like six or seven stories tall —"

"Ten stories tall," the Mad Mask said triumphantly. "The Mad Mask . . . er, I prefer nice, round numbers. And small feet."

Kyle was blown away. The sheer size of the robot . . . He had imagined something human-size, maybe a little bigger. Ten feet tall *at the most*. But this thing . . . It would be taller than anything else in Bouring, including the very lighthouse right next to them.

"How . . ." He stopped himself before he stuttered again, clearing his throat. "How did you design this? Why did you even come up with this in the first place?"

The Mad Mask planted his fists on his hips and tilted his face (er, mask) dramatically toward the sun, which obligingly cast a glowing black sheen over the ebony wood. "Once," he intoned, "the Mad Mask was a child, much as yourself, living, toiling in obscurity and anonymity. And then, one day as you may have heard, the stars fell down in this very town, not far from here."

The plasma storm! Kyle thought, excited. Of course, if it boosted his own intellect, why couldn't it do so to the Mad Mask, too? But he hadn't seen anyone at the football field that night, so how . . .

"In the days following that astronomical event," the Mad Mask went on, "I journeyed to this town, my curiosity piqued. Although there were warning signs and police tape around the area in question, that could not stop such as I from a meeting with . . . my destiny!

"I explored the sports field where the stars had fallen down! And while I found nothing there, something clearly found *me*. For in the days that followed, my intelligence doubled, then doubled again and again!"

"It's exactly what happened to you!" Erasmus said in Kyle's ear.

Yeah, except it made him smarter, if these plans are any indication, Kyle thought sourly.

As if he could read Kyle's mind (and, in a way, he could, since they shared brain patterns), Erasmus whispered, "But he didn't get superpowers, and you did."

That was true. Being strong and fast and invulnerable and not bound to Earth wasn't a bad consolation prize.

He tuned back in to the Mad Mask's story, still in progress.

". . . such largesse, however, did not — could not — come without a price. And a most horrible price it was, Azure Avenger!" Here the Mad Mask got choked up. He bent over, cradling his mask in both hands. "The radiation did more than increase my intellect. It also . . . horribly disfigured me!"

It did what?

Kyle couldn't believe it. Now it all made sense — the beautifully crafted, lovingly carved mask wasn't just to protect the Mad Mask's true identity, like Kyle's hood; it was there as a new face, to replace the one that was destroyed by the radiation. Those feelings of jealousy he'd had a moment ago suddenly seemed immature and pathetic. Kyle had rolled the dice with the plasma curtain's radiation and come up with a greatly enhanced brain and superpowers. The Mad Mask had gotten better smarts, sure . . . but he also could never show his face to the world again.

Yikes.

"What did it . . . do to you?" Kyle asked. Some part of him wanted to know — he was curious, he couldn't help it — but he also hoped that the Mad Mask wouldn't pull of the mask and show him. It was probably pretty gross.

The Mad Mask straightened, his spine ramrod stiff. "We shall not speak of it!" he proclaimed. "The Mad Mask has only one face now!" He rapped the wooden mask with his knuckles, producing a hollow *glock-glock* sound. "Doctors could do nothing for me. My parents turned away from me. This face shall now suffice!"

"Thus devastated," he went on, continuing his story, "I fashioned a mask to hide my hideous visage from the prying eyes of a cold, uncaring world and swore most sacred revenge against beauty itself! Now, with your help, I will complete Ultitron and destroy all that is beautiful in the world!"

"Wow." It was all Kyle could think of to say. Destroy beauty? Really? That was the Mad Mask's goal? It seemed like a waste of time to Kyle, but if the Mad Mask wanted to blow up a couple of museums and trash a state park, he could do it. Kyle had more important things to worry about.

"Yes," the Mad Mask said, nodding. "Wow, indeed, Azure Avenger. Wow, indeed."

"Kyle," Erasmus whispered, "we have a problem."

"What?" Kyle asked automatically, forgetting that the Mad Mask couldn't hear Erasmus.

71

"I said, 'Wow, indeed,'" the Mad Mask clarified.

"Mighty Mike is on his way," said Erasmus.

Erasmus's Wi-Fi range was limited, but Kyle had installed a police scanner chip recently. It helped keep him apprised of the movement of the police so that he could avoid any unpleasant encounters.

"Apparently someone saw us and called the cops, who — predictably — called you-know-who," Erasmus went on, talking over the Mad Mask, who was now describing the difficulties he was having with Ultitron's motion controller unit.

"We have to get out of here," Kyle interrupted. "Now."

"The Mad Mask does not appreciate such rudeness."

"I'm sorry, Mad Mask, but Mighty Mike is on his way. He'll be here in just a few —"

"The Mad Mask fears no one — man, woman, child, or platypus!"

"Platypus?"

"Have you ever *seen* a platypus?" The Mad Mask shivered. "They're *freaky*."

"Well . . ." Kyle nervously checked the sky.

"And yet, the Mad Mask does not fear them! Nor does he fear Mighty —"

"Good to know," Mighty Mike said, swooping in from the top of the lighthouse. Kyle jumped back a step.

"Run!" he shouted to the Mad Mask. At the same instant Erasmus shouted, "Run!" so loudly that Kyle yelped and slapped a hand to his ear.

"The Mad Mask runs from no one!"

"Then stand right there!" Mighty Mike said, and plunged from the sky, his fists leading the way. Kyle reflexively flinched, but Mike was headed for the Mad Mask first. He slammed into the taller boy and . . .

KRACK-A-WHOOM!

The air itself exploded with a flash of hot white light, the sound of a thunderclap resounding as the Mad Mask's force field activated, flinging Mike backward heels-over-cape into the woods behind the lighthouse.

"Whoa . . ." Kyle could hardly believe what he was seeing. The Mad Mask had just delivered a massive smackdown to the alien punk. It was the most awesome thing ever.

A moment later, a large piece from a dead tree trunk hurtled out of the woods, aimed right at the Mad Mask. But Mike's aim was off — the tree was going to miss the Mad Mask and slam into the lighthouse instead. Kyle dived for it, knocking it aside before it could smash into the walls Mairi's mom had so carefully and lovingly restored.

"Be careful!" Kyle yelled. "Watch the property damage!"

"Watch your own property damage!" Mike yelled

back, soaring out of the woods and flying straight at Kyle.

"That doesn't even make any sense!"

A moment later, the talking stopped as Mike slammed into Kyle. They traded punches for a second or two and then the Mad Mask stepped in, grappling Mike from behind.

Mighty Mike shouted in pain as the force field crackled around him. Kyle jumped back just in case the force field couldn't tell the difference between him and Mighty Mike.

"You have to move this along," Erasmus said in Kyle's ear. "We're too close to the lighthouse. With all this energy and superstrength . . ."

He didn't need to finish. Kyle understood. He wished he had Mighty Breath like Mike did — then he could just blow Mike and the Mad Mask away from the lighthouse. But he would have to find another way.

He picked up the dead tree trunk Mike had flung so carelessly.

"Fisticuffs!" the Mad Mask chortled, punching Mike in the face as Mike grimaced. "Who knew physical combat could be so exhilarating!"

"Duck!" Kyle shouted, swinging the tree trunk.

"Duck? Duck-billed *platypus* —"

The Mad Mask was cut off as the tree trunk smashed into him. Kyle hissed in a sharp breath and winced at the impact. Oops.

Fortunately, the force of the blow made the Mad Mask collide with Mike, who stumbled back a few steps. The Mad Mask seemed unharmed, his force field still protecting him. Kyle replanted his feet and hefted the trunk again, ready to take another swing at Mike.

But before he could crack the alien on the head, Mike's eyes flashed black and the tree dissolved into melting goo in Kyle's hands. As Mighty Mike turned his gaze to Kyle, Kyle felt a tingling sensation along his neck and face.

Oh, no! That black vision of Mike's couldn't hurt Kyle — but it could destroy his mask!

Kyle dodged the black beams and watched a shallow scar sizzle its way along the wall of the lighthouse.

"Now look what you've done!" he told Mike.

"You shouldn't have moved!" Mike complained.

Kyle threw himself at Mike, determined to stop him before he caused more damage to the lighthouse. At the same moment, the Mad Mask swung a fist. They both connected with Mike at the same time, throwing him back into the woods.

"That won't hold him for long," Kyle said. "We need to —"

"Flee, my ally!" the Mad Mask said. He shoved the slate into Kyle's hand.

"But . . ."

"Flee!" The Mad Mask grabbed Kyle's arm and pushed him away from the melee. "I will cover your escape! We shall meet again — soon!"

For a moment, Kyle couldn't move, rooted to the spot. It made sense to get the heck out of here before Mike grabbed him or ripped off his mask or something like that, but he didn't want to just leave the Mad Mask in the lurch like this.

"He said go!" Erasmus yelled. "Quick! Before Mike recovers."

Kyle moved as fast as he could, grabbing his backpack and then taking off at top speed. He stayed low to the ground so that no one could see him. Just before he disappeared into the trees, he heard the Mad Mask shout, "Yes! Come again, Mighty Mike! Test your pitiful brawn against the brainpower of . . . the Mad Mask!"

Wow.

Kyle's escapes were always spectacular, he reminded himself. What could be more spectacular than bulleting away from a throwdown between his hated nemesis and his . . . his . . .

His most powerful ally.

He weaved through the trees until he couldn't hear the battle anymore, then cut to the east, whcre he knew the highway intersected with Major Street just outside of Bouring. The billboard that said YOU ARE ABOUT TO ENTER THE TOWN OF BOURING — IT'S NOT BORING! as well as THE HOME OF MIGHTY MIKE! loomed ahead. Landing just out of sight of the highway, Kyle quickly switched outfits, stuffing his costume into his backpack. After a moment's thought, he added the Mad Mask's electronic slate. He would have to figure out how to return it.

Hefting his backpack on both shoulders, Kyle walked home. He still couldn't believe what he'd seen. The Mad Mask was completely fearless, totally unafraid of Mighty Mike. Not that Kyle was afraid of Mike — he was just afraid of what Mike could do to him. Kyle knew that if he wasn't careful, it would be all too easy for Mike to rip off his mask in a tussle and reveal his identity to the world. So Kyle preferred not to mix it up with Mike physically. Although he had to admit — the few times he'd punched Mike, it had felt *really* good!

But the Mad Mask didn't care about being unmasked or getting hurt or anything. It made Kyle rethink his method of operation so far. Maybe he could be a bit . . . bolder.

At home, he went down into the basement. There on a shelf was his first (and so far, only) trophy as the Azure Avenger: a heavy, leaded stoppered jar filled with dirt.

This was no ordinary dirt, though. As Kyle turned the jar over in his hands, the dirt pulsated with a faint glow. When he held it up to his ear, he could hear a slight high-pitched whine. This dirt had come from the spot on the Bouring Middle School football field where the plasma curtain had touched down, bringing Mighty Mike to Earth and giving Kyle his powers.

And, apparently, scarring the Mad Mask for life.

Mighty Mike had a lot to answer for, Kyle thought. His arrival on Earth had caused all sorts of problems already, like the ASE that almost killed Mairi. It was a tough situation — if Mike hadn't come to Earth, then Kyle wouldn't have his powers and his heightened intelligence. So there was a bit of good from Mike's arrival. But all things being equal, Kyle would rather have things the way they used to be. He would give up his powers in an instant if it meant no Mighty Mike. But that was just a dream. Things weren't going to get any better unless Kyle did something about it.

He dragged an old lawn chair over to his workbench and flicked on the overhead lamp, then settled in with the electronic slate. He couldn't believe the sheer size and complexity of Ultitron. There was over a thousand gigabytes of information on its elbow alone. This was going to be a massive undertaking.

"The plans are . . . complicated, to say the least," Erasmus said.

"Did you grab them all?"

"Yes. I've downloaded them all to my hard drive. Speaking of which . . . I think I'm going to need an upgrade if you want me to hold on to all this data. It's getting a little crowded in here."

Kyle sighed. He would have to go steal a bigger hard drive. He would rather buy one, but his allowance had run out on the last round of upgrades for Erasmus. Being a pioneer in the field of artificial intelligence was tough on the wallet.

"All right. I'll see what I can do. What do you think of these plans?"

Erasmus hesitated before answering. "Well, realize that I haven't had time to go through all of them yet . . ."

"Spit it out."

"I don't get it." Kyle knew it pained the AI to admit this because it also pained him to admit it. "The Mad Mask must be several generations ahead of us in terms of robotics, cybernetics, artificial intelligence, fuzzy logic programming. . . . Makes me wonder, Kyle: Why does he need *your* help?"

Kyle nodded thoughtfully, flicking through screens on the slate. "Because working together, we can finish this thing faster than him working alone. Duh. Even he can only work so fast."

"I don't know . . ."

"I have to admit: It's nice to have another genius around. Someone I can talk to, maybe."

"Hey!"

"Don't be offended, Erasmus. You're patterned on my own brain waves. It's not the same."

The AI went into a sulky electronic silence.

"Still . . ." Kyle mused, tapping the slate, where a blueprint of Ultitron's right hand appeared. "All of this work in service of what? Destroying beauty? I guess it makes sense. . . ."

The more he thought about it, the more sense it made. Destroying beauty was a perfectly valid goal, he decided. The world was so superficial. Kyle knew that already. People became famous just because they were good-looking, even if they hadn't done anything to deserve it. That didn't seem right. Shouldn't people be famous for *doing* something, not for *being* something? What did a beautiful person contribute to the world? Something nice to look at? Who cared?

In a way, the Mad Mask's philosophy jibed with Kyle's. The Prankster Manifesto, after all, said that people took themselves too seriously and had to be pranked in order to understand that they weren't worthy of being taken so seriously. Similarly, the Mad Mask was trying to show the world that beauty was nothing worth having, that what mattered was . . .

"What matters is what's inside," Kyle muttered. It was a simplistic formula, one that his parents had told him since he was young. And yet it was undeniably true.

He flicked to another screen. Then another. And another. Absorbing the schematics. He would help the Mad Mask. Together, they would finish Ultitron and destroy Mighty Mike. And then . . . Then they would go about the even more difficult task of teaching the world how to be a better place.

In the end, maybe they wouldn't just be allies. Maybe they would also be . . . friends.

CHAPTER
EIGHT

The next day, Bouring Middle School buzzed with the news: There was a new "bad guy" in town! Mighty Mike had found him and the Blue Freak planning to blow up the lighthouse and stopped them. Unfortunately, they got away. But at least Mike saved the lighthouse.

Kyle tried to block out the buzz, seething. Even though it was against school rules, he slipped Erasmus's earbuds in whenever he could, just to block out the chatter. But he knew what people were saying.

Blow up the lighthouse? Idiots! He and the Mad Mask had no such plans. Where did people come up with this stuff?

The school gossip mill was good for one thing, at least — it filled Kyle in on what happened after he left Mike and the Mad Mask to pummel each other. Apparently, the Mad Mask staved off Mike's attacks with his force field, then used a variation of Kyle's laser-chaff to blind Mike and make good his escape. From the sound of it, he'd improved the laser-chaff in a number of ways, including mounting a firing mechanism in one of his gauntlets. Kyle liked that idea — he could spray laser-chaff wherever he pointed his fingers. He told Erasmus to start working on schematics for that.

"*Crowded* in here . . ." Erasmus complained.

"I'll get you a bigger hard drive soon, I promise."

Kyle was so happy that the Mad Mask had used his idea that he wasn't even upset at being ripped off. They were allies, right? Allies helped each other; they shared. The Mad Mask was going to let Kyle use Ultitron, so the least Kyle could do was let him use the laser-chaff idea.

The day would have been in balance between the buzz and the happiness Kyle felt at having met his new friend if not for Mairi.

She was still angry at him. On the bus, she had refused to sit next to him. And when he approached her after getting off the bus, she just snorted, turned away, and stomped off into school. Kyle did not like this behavior at all, but he wasn't sure what he could do about it. He was willing to apologize to Mairi, but if she wasn't willing to listen . . . Well, then everything was her fault, really. If she wouldn't listen to his apology, that was her fault, not his.

Still, he felt unsettled all day. Usually, he and Mairi would talk throughout the day, making snarky comments and rolling their eyes at each other whenever someone did or said something stupid (which was always). But today she ignored him.

His unsettled feeling lasted until after lunch (which he ate alone in a corner as Mighty Mike entertained an overflowing table of kids with the story of how he chased away two "bad guys" at once), when he went to gym class. Mairi wasn't in Kyle's gym class, but Mike was. Kyle had always hated gym, and now he hated it even more. And today, he would hate it even *more* than more.

"This is Physical Fitness Week!" Mr. Rogers, the gym teacher, announced as everyone groaned. Kyle joined in the groaning. Physical Fitness Week! That was the worst. As boring as gym class usually was, at least it was never demanding — they ran around and played soccer or volleyball or baseball or touch football. Pointless, but sort of fun and not annoying.

But during Physical Fitness Week, they would have to do exercises and keep track of their "progress" for the week. This would be done in front of everyone, meaning that for one class a day for the week, Kyle would spend most of his time sitting and watching someone else do sit-ups and push-ups and pull-ups and all that nonsense. When it was his turn, he would have to be careful not to reveal his powers. *Great.* One more thing on his mind. (Kyle's mind, of course, was enormous, but that didn't mean he wanted lots of useless clutter junking up the place. He liked a nice, neat, orderly mind.)

"Mike," Mr. Rogers said, "you, of course, are exempt from Physical Fitness Week."

Kyle gnashed his teeth. Of course Mike would get a pass on Physical Fitness Week. Everyone just *had* to bend over backward for that little punk. Look at him, standing there in his T-shirt and gym shorts, pretending to be like everyone else. A "Gosh, really?" expression plastered on his face.

"Really, Mr. Rogers?" Mike said with a syrupy innocence that made Kyle gag. "Gosh, I don't want specific treatment. I'm willing to prove I'm as fat as anyone else here."

Kyle barked a laugh at Mike's typical word-mangling, but no one else laughed — they just all looked over at Kyle with narrowed eyes, as if he'd just farted. He shrugged.

"I think you mean 'as *fit*,'" Mr. Rogers said. *And "special" treatment, not "specific,"* Kyle thought. Why didn't anyone notice that?

"But," Mr. Rogers went on, "there's no point in having you do any of these exercises. Anyone can see that you're very fit." Everyone stared at Mike, who was — Kyle had to admit — the sort of physical specimen you usually only saw in comic books and in animated movies. "And I don't think you'd find the exercises very difficult."

"I'd like to try," Mike said. "I want to be like no one else."

"Everyone else," you demented freak!

"It's not carnivalistic to treat me differently. Just since I have powers, you're all subsuming that I can exercise these performances. I should have to acquit myself like everyone else," Mike finished with a triumphant nod.

There were so many mangled expressions in that little speech that Kyle's head hurt.

"Well, okay, let's give it a shot." Mr. Rogers started calling kids up to the various stations to do exercises. Each kid was paired with a partner who would watch their form and count their reps. Kyle's partner was a kid named Luke who kept pumping his forearms and saying, "I'm huge! I'm huge!" Then he would grunt and do one of the exercises, shouting out the numbers. Every now and then Kyle would throw in a wrong number, just to mess up the count.

"One! Two! Three! Four!" Luke heaved, down on the floor doing push-ups. "Five! Six! Seven! Eight!"

"Thirteen!" Kyle said.

"Fourteen! Fifteen! Wait a sec." Luke paused, still on the floor, and looked at Kyle. "Where was I?"

"Eight," Kyle said.

Luke stared for a moment. Kyle imagined he could see the rusty gears of Luke's mental machinery slowly grinding.

"Nine!" Luke yelled, doing another push-up. "Ten!"

Kyle yawned. He realized that even though Luke was yelling his numbers ("Fifteen!" he shouted. "Twelve!" Kyle said. "Thirteen!" Luke bellowed) he was still having trouble hearing him. Slowly, he realized why.

Smack in the middle of the gym, Mighty Mike was doing push-ups, too. Only he was doing them at nearly blinding speed. His partner — a kid named Doug — was rattling off numbers as quickly as he could, but Kyle could tell he'd lost the rhythm awhile back. Everyone else was standing around, ignoring their own exercises and partners, chanting, "Go! Go! Go!" so loudly that Kyle couldn't hear his own breathing.

Mike obliged them. He was well past a hundred push-ups, the show-off, and showed no signs of tiring.

"Look at him!" a girl — Danika — said, her voice hushed with awe. "Look at those arms and shoulders!"

Kyle had to admit Mike's chiseled torso and arms were pretty impressive. Then again, when you were built by a plasma storm from another planet, you could probably dictate exactly what your body would look like. He wondered if there was some kind of menu: Choose from the following: A) Shoulders of Steel, B) Killer Lats, C) Six-Pack Abs, D) All of the Above.

Ha. One more reason to hate Mighty Mike. He hadn't worked hard for his physique. It just happened for him and to him. But here he was, showing off in front of everyone like he'd earned it.

"Is that enough?" he asked Mr. Rogers, popping up to his feet. The crowd applauded.

"That'll do," Mr. Rogers said, grinning. "Now, look, everyone — I don't expect any of you to be able to do what Mike here can do. But he's setting a good example. Try your hardest and you'll be able to do some mighty impressive things."

Kyle wanted to puke. No matter how hard any of these kids tried and trained and practiced and struggled, none of them would ever be able to achieve what Mighty Mike could do, by sheer dint of his alien origins and nothing else. Mr. Rogers was an idiot. Kyle would have to figure out a way to teach him a lesson in humility and common sense. The Prank Wheels started turning in his head.

They moved on to a new exercise: chin-ups. Mighty Mike did a hundred of them in a minute as the class watched in awe, his body a blur of motion as he hoisted and lowered himself on the bar over and over again. Everyone (except for Kyle) counted out loud as quickly as possible. One girl actually passed out from all the drama.

When it was Kyle's turn on the chin-up bar, he was keenly aware of all eyes on him, especially the eyes of Mighty Mike. The fainting girl had been revived by now and Kyle couldn't suppress a little private chuckle at the thought of *him* suddenly doing a hundred chin-ups in a minute. What a shock that would be — she would definitely faint again.

But, of course, he didn't dare.

As everyone watched, he gripped the chin-up bar with both hands, aware of how flimsy it felt. It was made out of polished steel and could hold hundreds of pounds, but to Kyle it felt like a hollow tube of aluminum foil. He could crumple it one-handed.

Mighty Mike watched him. Kyle took a deep breath and pulled himself up for a count of one.

"Whoa!" Mr. Rogers called out. "Save some energy there, Camden! Don't put it all into the first one. Pace yourself."

Titters from the class. Kyle had pulled himself up too quickly and confidently. He gritted his teeth and did it again for a two-count, this time deliberately going more slowly. It felt like swimming through syrup. It was like moving in slo-mo when all he wanted to do was go as fast as he could.

"Better!" Mr. Rogers called out. "We can't all be Mighty Mike, you know."

Kyle hung for a second from the bar, gathering his patience. If he tried to pull himself up right now, he would bend the bar, he knew.

"Just two?" Mr. Rogers said. "C'mon, Camden. You can do better than that." More laughter.

Kyle held his breath, his heart pumping wildly. He

didn't know what to do. He was so angry and embarrassed and . . . and . . . *angry* that he could feel his muscles tensing and bunching all up and down his arms and shoulders. If he exerted himself at all, he would crush the bar with his bare hands. But if he didn't move —

"All right, that's it, then," Mr. Rogers said. "Two. Not good, Camden. Something to work on."

"No, wait!" Kyle said. "I was just catching my breath. I can do more."

"Sure you can. C'mon. Down from the bar."

"But I can do more!" Kyle protested. He did a quick chin-up, holding back with all his focus and concentration. Success! He completed his third without mangling the bar. "See?"

"Very impressive," Mr. Rogers said in a tone that did not reflect anything "impressive" at all. He slapped Kyle on the back. "Hop down. We have to get through more people today."

"But —"

"Seriously," Mr. Rogers said with a shift from his pal-sy, jock-buddy voice to his I-am-your-teacher voice. He smacked Kyle on the hip with his clipboard, lightly.

Kyle lashed out without thinking of it. His foot came up and flailed artlessly at Mr. Rogers. It only struck him a glancing blow on the meatiest part of his shoulder (which, for Mr. Rogers, was extremely meaty), but that was enough to knock him off his feet and send him sprawling a couple yards away across the gym floor, sliding along on his butt until he collided with the bleachers.

Kyle dropped down from the chin-up bar into absolute silence. In less than the blink of an eye, Mighty Mike had arrived at Mr. Rogers's side. "Don't try to get up," he advised Mr. Rogers. "You could be interred."

"You mean 'injured'!" Kyle told him from the middle of the room.

Mr. Rogers rubbed his shoulder and glared at Kyle. "Camden," he said, "shut up."

Kyle fumed, his arms crossed defensively over his chest. "It was an *accident*," he said for the fifth time. "I didn't *mean* to do it."

"I know that," said Kyle's Great Nemesis (a.k.a. Melissa Masterton, Bouring Middle School's guidance counselor). Kyle was in her office, sitting across the desk from her. "I know that you would never *try* to hurt someone. But sometimes, Kyle, people get hurt even when we're not trying to hurt them. Do you think," she sing-songed, "that that's a lesson you might have learned today in gym class?"

Kyle rolled his eyes. The Great Nemesis's insane and inane burbling had haunted him throughout his tenure at

Bouring Elementary School, where she had recognized his great intellect and pranksterish tendencies pretty much on Day One. He'd thought he would escape her well-meaning, intrusive claptrap when he graduated to middle school, but she had transferred to Bouring Middle at the same time. Kyle figured she had taken a blood oath to make his life miserable. And that he could look forward to seeing her at Bouring High School in a few years.

"It was," Kyle said through clenched teeth, settling in for his sixth attempt, "an accident. Therefore, there's no lesson to learn. By definition, accidents can't be predicted. Ergo, they can't be effective teaching tools because they're non-repeatable. Any scientist could tell you this."

"Ergo?" the Great Nemesis said brightly, perking up. Her heavily eyeshadowed eyes widened. With her over-painted face and bright red lips, she looked like a fast-food drive-thru clown. Only less thoughtful and intelligent. "That's a pretty big word, Kyle. See, that's what I'm talking about. Someone with your intelligence should know better than to lash out like that. You know that could lead to someone being hurt. Now, in this case, that gym floor was very slippery, so Mr. Rogers went a lot farther than he should have. Still — you can't go around kicking people."

"First of all, *ergo* isn't a big word. It's only four letters. I think what you meant to say was that it's impressive for someone of my age to know and use Latinate words properly. I'll concede that. But in no way is it a 'big word.' Second of all, I only kicked out of reflex because Mr. Rogers kept smacking me with his clipboard. And he was humiliating me in front of everyone."

As soon as he said "humiliating," Kyle knew he'd made a huge mistake. Stuff like that — "feelings" and "social pressures" — were like fresh, bleeding chum to the shark that was the Great Nemesis.

Sure enough, her eyes lit up and her mouth made an almost perfect O — as in, *Oh, goody! Now I can talk about Kyle's feelings!*

"Oh, Kyle. Kyle. I understand. This is such a difficult age. And to be embarrassed in front of your friends like that, well, it must have been very trying." She leaned on the desk with her elbows and smiled a horrifying smile. "Let's talk about those feelings, okay?"

Kyle groaned and put his face in his hands.

"It was an *accident*!" he said for the seventh (and, he was sure, *not* the last) time.

CHAPTER
NINE

As the week wore on, Kyle tried to assuage his feelings by reverting to the one thing that always made him feel good: pranks.

Mairi still wasn't talking to him and a bunch of kids had taken to calling him "Mighty Weak" (which didn't rhyme with "Mighty Mike," so it was a bad and insipid pun). So on Tuesday, he decided that every toilet in the school would simultaneously overflow.

Every.

Single.

Toilet.

All at once.

This would accomplish a couple of things: It would make Kyle feel better (most important, of course), but it would also catch any number of kids off guard, furnishing them with their own embarrassing moments that would make his embarrassing moment in gym class fade from everyone's memories. To this end, he developed a special chemical compound that would, when released into the school's plumbing, spread itself out, diffusing through the pipes and then — at a pre-timed interval — change its own chemical configuration, immediately backing up the toilets and causing an overflow that would (in nine out of ten computer models designed by Erasmus) be quite explosive.

The thought of water simultaneously shooting out of the forty-two toilets and twenty-seven urinals at Bouring Middle School, into the surprised and unsuspecting faces and rear ends of any number of students and teachers, made Kyle laugh so hard that he thought he pulled a muscle.

But at lunchtime, as he slipped away from the cafeteria to an isolated bathroom in order to dump his vial of chemicals into the pipes, who should show up? Mighty Mike! Yes, the do-gooder brat just happened to have to use the bathroom at the same time. And even though Kyle was in a stall with the door closed, Mike managed to push the stall door open at the worst possible moment, jostling Kyle's arm and making him spill the chemicals on the floor instead of into the toilet.

"Oh. Hoops. I'm sorry," Mike said.

"It's not 'hoops.' It's 'whoops.' Or 'oops,'" Kyle corrected him automatically, while watching his awesome (and rare) chemicals spread out across the tile floor. He'd had to steal several of the compounds, and he couldn't risk doing it again.

"Are you sure?" Mike asked. "It's not 'hoops'?"

Kyle pushed past him and left the bathroom.

The next day, he decided to go simple: He whipped up a little audio device that he patched into the school PA system. Now, at utterly random moments, the school PA would make a farting sound. It didn't matter if someone was talking on it or if the system was turned off. At random moments, the PA was going to fart, whether the school liked it or not.

It was juvenile, yes, but Kyle didn't care at this point. He just wanted to exercise his prank muscles and do something that would get kids to stop gossiping about his weak performance on the chin-up bar.

Sure enough, toward the end of first period the PA crackled to life and made a halfhearted farting sound before it suddenly died. Instead of laughter or chatter, all the sound did was cause the kids to look at each other in confusion and then shrug.

The bell rang almost immediately, so Kyle dashed to the janitor's closet on the first floor, where he'd patched into the PA system through an electrical switchbox. Mighty Mike was standing there already, a confused look on his face, holding Kyle's audio device. The wire that connected it to the PA was snapped.

"Whoops," Mike said, then smiled up at Kyle. "Hey, you're right! 'Whoops' *does* sound better!" He clenched his fist, crushing the audio player. "Whoops!" He laughed. "Yeah, definitely whoops! This thing made a weird noise. I could hear over it even from herstory class."

Mike beamed with pride, so thrilled with himself for figuring this out that he didn't even think to ask what Kyle was doing in the janitor's closet.

"History" class, Kyle thought. *And "overhear." You idiot.*

So. At school, he was a failure and a laughingstock. At home, he was doing no better. Despite spending hours poring over the Mad Mask's schematics, Kyle still couldn't grasp them. Ultitron was the most confusing, confounding thing Kyle had ever imagined in his life. And this was coming from the guy who had built the now-legendary Pants Laser.

"This just doesn't make any sense!" he told Lefty one night. He was sprawled out on his bed, the slate before him, Lefty similarly sprawled out nearby, nose twitching. Kyle rubbed the rabbit's ear between his thumb and forefinger — sometimes that calmed both of them.

"The data intake module can't connect here," he went on, pointing to the slate. "It conflicts with the ocular synthesis systems over here. That means its eyes," he explained to Lefty, who cocked an eye at Kyle and twitched his nose wisely.

"This system was either designed by an idiot or a certified genius," Erasmus chimed in, scrutinizing the copy of the schematics on his own hard drive. "There are power couplings that attach directly to networking nodes, servomechanisms that don't have any sort of internal or external structural support. . . . It just doesn't make any sense."

Kyle agreed. But every time he wanted to throw away the schematics in disgust, he thought of the Mad Mask's force field. That thing *definitely* worked; there was no question about it. If that same genius was being applied to Ultitron, then Kyle couldn't just dismiss the blueprints, no matter how big a headache they gave him.

On Thursday, he spied Mairi sitting alone at lunch. He bought two pizzas — one sausage, one pepperoni — so that they could share, like they always used to do on Thursdays. He approached her hesitantly. They hadn't talked in almost a week. If he hadn't had the distractions of trying to come up with a great prank and studying the Mad Mask's impossible schematics, it would have driven him crazy. As it was, it still nagged at the back of his brain, like someone softly poking his shoulder over and over, not hard, but just enough that he could feel it.

He approached her quietly. She had her backpack on the table and she was reading a book, so she didn't notice him standing there until he cleared his throat loudly.

She looked up at him and didn't say anything for what felt like a long, long time, but Kyle knew was only three seconds. Then, without a word, she slid her backpack off the table.

And revealed a lunch tray with two pizzas on it: one pepperoni, one sausage.

Kyle couldn't help it — he laughed. Mairi smiled a very wide smile. "I guess we both had the same idea," she said.

Kyle sat down across from her, and even though they already each had a sausage and a pepperoni pizza, they still went through the age-old ritual of cutting each pizza in half and swapping plates. Kyle contentedly bit into the pepperoni first, then the sausage, going back and forth with each bite.

They ate in silence, and then Mairi said, "I'm not stupid."

Kyle froze. "I . . . I never said you were." But he felt guilty anyway. The fact of the matter was that — compared to Kyle — just about everyone in the world *was* stupid. Except for the Mad Mask, of course. But everyone *else*. And, yeah, that included Mairi. It's not that she was stupid — it's just when you put her brainpower up against Kyle's . . . it was no contest. That wasn't her fault. For a normal kid, Mairi was really, really smart. Kyle didn't want to think about it, really. He felt bad just having the conversation at all.

"I didn't say you said I was stupid," Mairi said, frowning. "Listen to what I'm saying, Kyle, not what you think I'm saying, all right? I'm saying: I'm not stupid. I see how you've been ever since Mike came to town. And I totally get it. You were the most popular kid in school. You were probably the most popular kid in the whole town. And then Mike came along and suddenly everyone's been paying a lot of attention to him. No one chants your name when you walk down the hall —"

"That was always annoying," Kyle said. But he had to admit, he missed it.

"I bet you miss it, though," Mairi said, eerily reading his mind. "I know I would miss it, if it had been me.

"But here's the thing, Kyle." She pointed her fork at him to drive her point home. "You can't blame Mike for any of this. None of it's his fault. He didn't ask for this to happen to him. He has near-total amnesia. No one's been able to figure out where he's from or who his parents are. His family is out there looking for him somewhere and he's all alone and even he can't remember who he is or where he came from."

He's from another planet, Kyle wanted to say, but couldn't.

"So he only has his foster parents," Mairi went on, "and the Matthewses are really nice, but he needs friends his own age, you know? That's where I come in. Because everyone else just wants him to fly them around or pick up their car or show how he can shoot those funky black beams out of his eyes. But he needs downtime, too. He needs to be able to be a kid. Because he *is* a kid."

He's an alien kid, is what he is. Kyle bit into the sausage pizza to cover up his uncontrollable look of disgust.

"So I guess what I'm saying is, maybe you should try to put yourself in his shoes. I know him being here has changed things for you, but at the end of the day, you get to go home and get into your own bed and you get to be with your own parents and play with Lefty and all that. It would be great if you could be friends with Mike. And if you can't do that, well . . ." She shrugged. "I understand if you can't do that, and I won't be angry at you. But if you can't be his friend, then at least maybe you can, I don't know, *not* be angry at me just because I *am* his friend."

She gazed at him across the table, her big green eyes wide and hopeful. Kyle couldn't bear to disappoint her, but there was also no way in this world or any other that he could promise to be Mighty Mike's — shudder — friend. So instead, he said:

"It'll all be all right, Mairi. Don't worry."

Which wasn't really saying anything at all, but it seemed to make her happy.

Kyle didn't know if he'd told the truth or told a lie. He figured he would find out eventually.

And so, that night, Mairi came over to the Camden house to work on the science project. Kyle took a deep breath and forced himself not to think about how simplistic the project was, especially when compared to his own "special science project" — the schematics for Ultitron. Instead, he decided to pretend for one night that he'd never been exposed to the radiation from the plasma curtain, that his IQ had never jumped into quadruple digits. For Mairi, he pretended to be the same old Kyle Camden he'd always been.

And it was fun! They avoided talking about Mighty Mike at all. Mom made some snacks for them, and they sat on the living room floor with their project spread out all around them — long chains of taped-together sheets of paper with shaky lines of varying crayon colors stretching as far as the eye could see. Mairi giggled at Kyle's insistence on trying to make the lines perfectly straight, while Kyle joked that her lines weaved all over the paper like their sleepy-eyed bus driver.

He went upstairs for Lefty, plopping the big rabbit down on the floor so that he could hop around. "Rabbits need exercise," Kyle said seriously, and Mairi nodded just as seriously. They both watched as Lefty — who apparently didn't know that rabbits needed exercise — yawned an enormous, pink-tongued yawn, his sharp front teeth huge in his mouth, and then flopped on his side on the carpet and proceeded to go to sleep.

Mairi and Kyle exchanged a look and burst into a fit of crazy giggles. Soon, they were poking Lefty lightly on his little cotton tail, trying to prod him awake so that he would do something. Anything.

"You're going to get fat, Lefty!" Mairi said.

"Your legs are going to fall asleep!" Kyle told him.

"All the girl bunnies won't be able to see your awesome six-pack abs under all the bunny blubber!"

"You'll get so fat you'll need one of those scooters the old people use on TV!"

"Your stomach will drag on the ground when you hop around!"

"You won't —" Kyle was interrupted by the doorbell. He checked the time. It was almost nine o'clock at night. Who would be coming over this late?

"Kyle!" Mom called from the TV room. "Get the door, please!"

"Can't you?" Kyle called back. "We're working!" Even though they hadn't done any work for the past ten minutes.

"No commercial!" Dad yelled, almost in a panic, as if he might miss five seconds of whatever he was watching.

Kyle rolled his eyes. He had given up on his parents ever remembering to use the DVR. So he got up to go to the door. Mairi gathered the lethargic Lefty into her lap and stroked his fur, telling him that he needed to take better care of himself.

Annoyed, Kyle stomped through the house to the front door and flung it open, expecting to see some clueless friend of his parents.

Instead, standing there on the front step, in his full costume, was the Mad Mask!

CHAPTER
TEN

Kyle stood at the front door, gaping, his mind spinning like a centrifuge. The Mad Mask! Right here! At his *home*! There weren't enough exclamation points in the entire universe to express Kyle's shock.

"What are you —"

"The Mad Mask told you we would meet again!" the Mad Mask boomed.

"Shh! Keep it down!" Kyle cast a panicked eye over his shoulder. Had his parents heard? Had Mairi?

"The Mad Mask told you we would meet again," the Mad Mask whispered.

"How did you — never mind. Get in here." He ushered the Mad Mask into the house and quickly shut the door. Fortunately, it had been dark outside for hours and most people in Kyle's neighborhood — heck, most people in Bouring — didn't wander the streets at all hours. He figured no one had spotted the Mad Mask standing . . .

On his front doorstep! Kyle resisted the urge to pull

at his hair — he was so freaked out that he would end up as bald as a bowling ball.

"Who is it?" Mom shouted from the TV room. For the first and only time in his life, Kyle was grateful that his parents stayed put once they settled into their TV-watching positions. Except for bathroom breaks.

"Girl Scout cookies!" Kyle yelled back.

"Did you tell them the usual?"

Kyle slapped his forehead. That's right. His parents had a standing order for Girl Scout cookies. Why hadn't he come up with a better lie? Now he would have to make sure he scored Girl Scout cookies somehow. "Yes!" he called to her. "You have to get out of here!" he whispered to the Mad Mask. "I have company!"

As if on cue, Mairi said, "Thin Mints! Thin Mints!" from the living room.

The Mad Mask clasped his hands behind his back and tilted his head this way and that, taking in the vestibule of the Camden house. "Typical post-recessionary American suburban construction," he said. Noticing the family portrait Mom had hung on the wall, he snickered. "Bourgeois 'art,' attempting to compensate for lack of taste and skill with highly suspect and generic emotional content."

"You really have to go," Kyle told him. "Do your teleport thingy and . . ." Kyle made a magician's *poof*ing gesture with both hands.

"The Mad Mask meant no insult by his art assessment," the Mad Mask said. "Indeed, the Mad Mask's mother indulges in similar interior decoratorial tragedies. Now" — he straightened — "let us begin our work."

"Haven't you been listening to me? I —"

"Kyle!" Mairi said from the other room. "If you're in the kitchen, get me a soda, too."

"Right!" he shouted, panicking. He grabbed the Mad Mask by the shoulders. "See?"

"I think Lefty just pooped!" Mairi called out.

Kyle groaned.

"Walls should be used to display art of worth and merit," the Mad Mask went on. "Or left blank, in which case they are useful to inscribe with equations and formulae. Maudlin tripe such as this, however," he went on, gesturing to the portrait, "shames and dishonors the character and potential of a good wall."

"Please leave," Kyle mumbled, certain at this point that there was nothing he could do to get the Mad Mask to go.

"Oh, yuck!" Mairi said, and Kyle's heart triple-timed as he realized her voice sounded louder — she was getting closer to him. She was coming here!

He opened the coat closet and — before the Mad Mask could say or do anything — shoved the Mad Mask inside and closed the door just as Mairi walked into the foyer.

"He *did* poop!" she said.

"Really?" Kyle hoped his panic didn't show. Fortunately, Mairi seemed preoccupied with Lefty's bowels and the products thereof. "You know, rabbit poop is small and dry and not a big deal. It looks the same coming out as it does going in."

"I just want to get a paper towel and pick it up off the carpet. Are you okay?" she asked suspiciously.

"I'm fine!" Kyle said, his voice squeaking. He shot a quick glance at the closet door.

Mairi's eyes narrowed. "What are you up to, Kyle?"

"Nothing! I swear!"

"Where's my soda? Have you been hanging out in the foyer the whole time?"

Kyle almost gave up right there. He couldn't win. He might as well just fling open the closet door and introduce Mairi to the Mad Mask.

"I . . ." he said, at a loss. "I was just going in there. Right this minute."

Something thumped in the coat closet. Kyle coughed loudly to try to cover it up.

Mairi looked at the closet door, then slowly turned to look at Kyle. "What's going on here?"

"Nothing at all," Kyle said. "Nothing in the slightest. Nothing." He wondered if he could cram the word *nothing* in there any more.

After giving the closet door one more glance, Mairi went into the kitchen. Kyle breathed a sigh of relief.

"Is that the time?" Mairi said from the kitchen. "I didn't realize it was so late!"

Kyle fist-pumped.

"Yeah, it's getting late," he said. The closet door opened and the Mad Mask handed Kyle Mairi's coat. Kyle grabbed it and slammed the closet door, spinning around just as Mairi emerged from the kitchen with a fistful of paper towels and a puzzled expression.

"Are you rushing me out of here?"

"No! Of course not! But it *is* getting late." He took the paper towels from her, transferring the coat to her at the same time. "Oh, that Lefty. I'll clean up after him. Thanks for the paper towels."

Mairi frowned but nodded. Kyle helped her into her coat, then opened the front door. "I'll see you tomorrow," he told her, gesturing outside and thinking, *Get out! Get out now!* while offering what he hoped was a casual and reassuring smile.

Mairi stepped outside, then paused before going down the front steps. "What about the project?" she asked. "We left a mess in the living room."

Kyle leaned outside, holding the door almost closed. "Don't worry. I'll take care of it." He chuckled hollowly and held up the paper towels. "And Lefty's poop, too."

Mairi looked like she was going to say something, but instead she just shrugged, waved, and headed home. Kyle waited a few seconds, in case she turned around, then quickly closed the front door and ran to the closet. He had to get the Mad Mask out of the house.

Pulling open the closet door, he saw . . . nothing.

Well, not *nothing* — there were coats in there. It was a coat closet, after all. But the Mad Mask was gone.

Kyle spun around, half expecting the masked teenager to be standing behind him, but all he saw was the family portrait that had so annoyed the Mad Mask.

He must have teleported away, Kyle thought. *Good!*

In the living room, Kyle picked up the bunny poop on the carpet and tossed the paper towel. Then he tucked Lefty under his arm. "You've exhausted my goodwill, young man. You're going back in your cage."

Lefty yawned expansively to show how much he cared.

Walking past the TV room on his way to the stairs, Kyle heard something that chilled his blood. A voice. It *couldn't* be . . .

But it was.

He poked his head into the TV room. Sure enough, the Mad Mask was standing right there! With Kyle's parents!

Fortunately, the Mad Mask was standing behind the sofa, and Kyle's parents were staring straight ahead at the TV, as if the secrets to life, happiness, and calorie-free chocolate cake flickered there in high-def. Lefty grunted as Kyle squeezed him without realizing it.

"Does this television program provide insight into interpersonal relationships," the Mad Mask was asking, "or does it simply exist to illustrate common perceptions and misperceptions vis-à-vis such artificial social constructs?"

"The fat people have to date the skinny people," Dad said.

"Or they don't win the prize," Mom added, her shoulder twitching from her exposure to Kyle's brain-wave manipulator.

"Indeed," said the Mad Mask, drawing himself up to his full height. "And what is the prize?"

"Plastic surgery!" Kyle's parents said at the same time.

Kyle was frozen to his spot, stuck in the archway that led into the TV room. From where he stood, Kyle could see his parents on the couch and the Mad Mask behind them at an angle. His parents must not have seen the Mad Mask enter, so enraptured were they with their TV show. As long as the Mad Mask stayed where he was — and as long as Mom and Dad didn't suddenly turn around — they wouldn't see anything. Now he had to get the Mad Mask out of the house without them noticing.

"Uh, hi," he said, finally forcing himself into the living room. "I see you've all, uh, met . . ."

"Ah!" The Mad Mask put his fists on his hips and boomed, "Welcome, Az —"

"As they say in Germany!" Kyle blurted out before the Mad Mask could finish saying *Azure Avenger.*

Everyone in the room looked at Kyle. Fortunately, the Mad Mask didn't move, so he was still behind Mom and Dad. Kyle's parents had baffled expressions on their faces, and Kyle imagined the Mad Mask looked the same under his mask.

"How — how do you mean?" Dad asked.

"They don't say 'welcome,' in Germany," Mom said, one eyelid fluttering.

Kyle's mind raced. He chuckled. "Well, of course they do! They just . . . They just say it in German, is all."

Silence. Then Mom nodded thoughtfully. "Yes, that's true."

It must have been a commercial break because his parents didn't automatically turn back to the TV. "We didn't know you were having another friend over to work on your science project." Mom said.

"Yeah," Dad chimed in. "What did you say your name was?"

Kyle knew the Mad Mask was about bellow *the Mad Mask* at the top of his lungs, so he jumped in right away. "Theodore! His name's Theodore."

"I knew a kid named Theodore," Dad commented. "We called him 'Dore.' Does anyone ever call you — Oh!" This exclamation because the TV show had come back on, shutting off both parents' brains.

Kyle took advantage of the distraction to grab the Mad Mask and haul him out of the TV room. They went down into the basement, where Kyle could finally let loose.

"What were you *thinking*?" he demanded. "You can't just come to my house dressed like that! Someone could see! No one knows I'm the Azure Avenger. You could ruin everything."

And — Kyle realized suddenly — the Mad Mask could have even led Mighty Mike right to his doorstep. If Mike had been flying overhead and recognized the Mad Mask and followed him . . . Oh, man! That would be a disaster.

The Mad Mask flipped a hand as if Kyle's concerns were just dust to be brushed away. He turned around and paced the basement floor, taking in various gadgets and projects Kyle had in differing states of completion. "While the Mad Mask comprehends your distress, it is ultimately meaningless. We have a greater destiny ahead of us."

"Don't you have parents? Aren't you worried about —"

"My parents forsook me when I was disfigured. They

turned their backs on me, refusing even to look at me or to speak of my tragic mutilation."

The Mad Mask related this in the flat, uninflected tones of someone who doesn't care, but Kyle couldn't believe that was the case. His own parents were annoying and none too smart, but Kyle still loved them. He would be devastated if they ever rejected him. One more reason the world could never know that Kyle Camden and the Azure Avenger were one and the same — it would destroy his parents.

"I'm really sorry to hear that," he started, but the Mad Mask once again flicked his hand dismissively.

"The past is the past. We are concerned with the future. Nothing less." He paused in his pacing near the biochemical forge. "And what is this?"

"That's my biochemical forge. I'm cultivating a species of —"

"Interesting," the Mad Mask said with a bored voice.

"Look, how did you even find me? I never told you who I was. I wore a mask . . ."

In his circumambulation of the basement, the Mad Mask had come to the workbench. He stopped there and picked up the electronic slate. Kyle groaned. He knew what the Mad Mask was about to say, so he said it for him.

"You had a tracking device in the slate, didn't you?" He could almost see the Mad Mask smiling, even with the mask on.

"There had to be a way to find you, so that we could begin our work," the Mad Mask said.

"But anyone could have answered the door. How did you know it was me? You've never seen me without my mask."

"Your height and general build do not change whether you are in or out of costume. Hence, the Mad Mask was able to deduce that — unless an identical twin lived in this house — you must, in fact, be you." He nodded curtly. "Which you are. You, that is."

Kyle gave up. He'd been outthought again. He would just have to deal with it. (And, he resolved, there was no way in the world he was going to tell Erasmus about this. The mocking would never end.)

"A question," the Mad Mask said, now standing near the time machine. "The lagomorph. Is it an experimental subject? Does it exist for breeding purposes? Or perhaps as a comestible?"

It took Kyle a moment to realize that he was talking about Lefty, who was now snoozing comfortably under Kyle's arm. "What?" Comestible . . . Oh, gross! "No, I'm not going to eat him! Lefty is my pet, not dinner." He cradled Lefty protectively, as though the Mad Mask were about to lunge at him with a pot and a family recipe for hasenpfeffer.

"A pet. How . . . plebeian." Before Kyle could object, the Mad Mask went on. "Still, all men of greatness and accomplishment have had their eccentricities. Your affectation and affection do not appear to interfere with your progress in the sciences, so the Mad Mask shall overlook them."

The Mad Mask rubbed his gloved hands together, and for a moment Kyle imagined that he could see his eyes gleaming even through the protective, reflective lenses in the mask. The basement light glinted off the ivory tear.

"And now . . ." the Mad Mask chortled, "we shall begin to construct . . . the future!"

"Kyle!" Dad yelled from the top of the basement steps. "It's almost ten o'clock! Get to bed!"

Kyle and the Mad Mask stared at each other in silence for a moment.

"On the morrow, then!" the Mad Mask crowed.

"On the morrow," Kyle agreed. "And whatever you do, don't tell anyone who I am or where I live. That would be a disaster." He showed the Mad Mask out through the basement door and told him to come back tomorrow once darkness fell. "Oh, yeah: And be sure to use this door, not the front door, got it?"

"It is, truly, gotten," said the Mad Mask.

Once he was alone, Kyle finally breathed easily. He held Lefty up in front of him, and as the rabbit blinked open its pinkish eyes, said, "That was way too close, Lefty." Then he tucked Lefty under his arm again and went upstairs.

"And don't worry," he added as an afterthought. "I would never eat you."

CHAPTER
ELEVEN

The next evening, Kyle was killing time in the basement, making a chart of Mighty Mike's latest exploits. He was looking for patterns to Mike's behavior, analyzing when and how he used his various superpowers, which mistakes he made when. And why. Anything that would give him an edge. He lost track of time, absorbed in thought, when — true to his word — the Mad Mask arrived as darkness fell, slipping into Kyle's basement silently.

"Since your workspace is pleasing," he announced, causing Kyle to blush with pleasure, "we shall commence our work here, rather than at the Mad Mask's lair."

Kyle flashed back to the enormous size of Ultitron from the schematics. "But — but there's no room for something that big here!"

"Do not cloud the conversation with petty details. We need no significant amount of room. The major construction on Ultitron is completed already. We merely need to develop, assemble, and perfect specific control modules. Those tasks can easily be accomplished here, with the finished components moved to my lair and installed once tested."

Well, that made sense. Kyle was a little concerned about working with the Mad Mask in his basement, though — his parents could decide to come downstairs. He asked the Mad Mask to work in regular clothes and without the mask.

"The Mad Mask's deformity shall never be revealed to the open air!" the Mad Mask cried. "This mask shall conceal the grotesquerie that was once a pleasing visage 'til the end of time itself!"

So, yeah, Kyle figured he wouldn't have any luck talking his ally out of that.

He decided to attack the problem from the other direction. If he couldn't get the Mad Mask to look normal for his parents, he would fix his parents instead. This meant going back to the brain-wave manipulator, one of the very first gadgets Kyle had built after receiving his amped-up intelligence from the plasma storm that brought Mighty Mike to Earth.

The brain-wave manipulator made Kyle feel a little nervous . . . and more than a little bit guilty. He'd used it on his parents without testing it and now they both had side effects. He didn't really want to use it again, but he didn't see how he had a choice. Marching up the stairs with the brain-wave manipulator tucked under his arm, he resolved to spend some time working on perfecting the device so that he could remove the side effects.

"Hey, guys," he said. "Got a sec?"

Both of his parents looked over at him from the kitchen table, where they were enjoying dinner. Kyle pointed the brain-wave manipulator and triggered it.

"You won't notice anything strange about my friend Theodore. He just seems like a normal kid to you. You don't mind that he wears a mask."

"Why — why would that bother us?" Dad asked, now stuttering on *why*, too.

"We love Theodore!" Mom chirped, and then made a clicking sound with her tongue.

Oh, boy. If he didn't fix the machine before he needed to use it again, he was going to turn his parents into total rejects.

As he rounded the corner to return to the basement, he nearly collided with the Mad Mask, who was lurking at the top of the stairs. In that moment of distraction, the Mad Mask was easily able to pluck the brain-wave manipulator from Kyle's hands.

"Do you mind?" the Mad Mask asked in a tone of voice that told Kyle that he didn't really care what the answer was.

Together they went into the basement. The Mad Mask opened the shoe box that held the brain-wave manipulator. Kyle felt a momentary flush of shame creep along his cheeks and back to his ears. He'd thrown together the brain-wave manipulator very quickly and hadn't spent any time on its aesthetics or style. It was just a bunch of gadgetry tossed into a shoe box so that he could carry it around without being asked questions. He hated the thought of being judged on this particular device, especially when he had so much more to show off.

But the Mad Mask merely poked around in the innards of the shoe box for a moment, then grunted in something like satisfaction. "This is a most impressive device you've constructed. It completely rewrites the subject's own mental drives?"

"Sort of." Kyle took the brain-wave manipulator back and cradled it protectively against his chest. The Mad Mask leaned toward it with an eagerness that bothered Kyle for some reason. "It adjusts alpha wave activity to stimulate brain chemistry, creating new memories and thoughts."

"Fascinating! The Mad Mask applauds your ingenuity." For a moment, Kyle thought he sensed that the Mad Mask was going to reach out to take the manipulator again. "With this device in your arsenal, why have you not enslaved the entire town of Bouring?"

Kyle opened his mouth to answer, then stopped. Enslave the entire town? He supposed something like that was possible, but what would be the point? He didn't want slaves; he wanted two very small, very simple things: 1) for people to stop being foolish, and 2) for people to reject Mighty Mike. For the first, he'd developed the Prankster Manifesto. For the second, he'd become the Azure Avenger. In both cases, compelling people by manipulating their brain waves wouldn't be nearly as satisfying as having them come around on their own and agree with Kyle of their own free will.

"I can't use it on anyone but my parents," Kyle said. "It only works on people genetically related to me."

The Mad Mask snorted. "Ah. Well. Perhaps not as impressive as originally assumed." Kyle thought his new ally might decide against their team-up, but then the Mad Mask gestured to the workbench and the electronic slate that lay there. "Let us commence! It is time for you to take your first step on the path to the future!"

"Yes!" Kyle set the brain-wave manipulator on the shelf next to the jar of irradiated soil he'd collected from the spot where Mighty Mike had touched down on Earth. "I can't wait to start working on the Ultitron."

Spinning around, the Mad Mask spat out, "It's just Ultitron! There's no 'the'! Ultitron! Ultitron!"

Kyle held up his hands. "Right. Right. Got it. Sorry. Slip of the tongue."

"Say it aloud!"

"Ultitron."

"Mighty Ultitron!"

"Mighty Ultitron."

"Magnificent Ultitron!"

"Magnificent Ultitron."

"*Glorious* Ultitron!" the Mad Mask roared.

"Glorious — Look, can we just get to work? It's late and my parents are going to poke their heads down here soon enough."

"Right."

Together, they settled in at the workbench and began poring over the schematics, a position they found themselves in for the next several days as they planned out the construction of the crucial control modules that would actually bring Ultitron to life. Kyle's parents would occasionally check on them, reminding them late at night that "It's time for Theodore to go home," but they never commented on the Mad Mask's mask and outfit, testament to the power of the brain-wave manipulator.

Kyle wondered — briefly — where the Mad Mask went when he wasn't in Kyle's basement. He had said that his parents no longer talked to him, so Kyle figured that he wasn't living at home anymore.

"He mentioned a lair of some sort," Erasmus said at one point. "He must have a hideaway somewhere."

"That's true . . ." Kyle mused.

"Maybe you should follow him one night. Find out where he goes."

Kyle was horrified by the idea. The Mad Mask was his partner. There was a trust between them, and he wouldn't violate that by sneaking around and stalking. He told Erasmus this, but the AI was one step ahead of him.

"He followed *you*, remember? Twice!"

"We weren't partners yet. He's been fine since we teamed up."

Erasmus grumbled, but Kyle took out the earbuds. He didn't feel like hearing it. He had more important things to do than listen to Erasmus complain.

At the same time he was assembling parts for Ultitron, Kyle had to work on his joint science project with Mairi. When the weekend came, he spent the days working with Mairi and the nights working with the Mad Mask; he was becoming more and more exhausted. Still, despite all his hard work, he felt that he wasn't making enough progress on Ultitron, so he started staying up late into the night after the Mad Mask had left, working on what his partner called "the motivational engine."

"It doesn't work!" he complained in the early hours of Sunday morning, his eyes bloodshot and his fingers trembling from hours of intricate wiring and soldering in the basement. He slammed a fist down, shaking and denting the workbench at the same time. "Why won't it work? I followed the schematic perfectly!"

In frustration, he nearly threw it across the room but checked himself. He couldn't lose his temper. The Mad Mask was counting on him. Kyle didn't want to disappoint his new ally. While he hated to admit it (and never would admit it to anyone but himself), there was so much he could learn from the Mad Mask. For starters, the secrets of the teleportation device and the force field that was so powerful it could repel even Mighty Mike.

"I have to get this working," he muttered to himself, bending over the motivational engine again. "Once Ultitron is finished, we can send it to wipe out Mighty Mike. That's what matters."

His fingers slipped as he tried to thread a wire into the engine, and Kyle found himself chuckling. "I'm so tired I'm even talking to myself. . . ."

Yawning, he went to his bedroom, tossed some yogurt drops into Lefty's cage, and fell into a short, dreamless sleep that ended when his mother woke him up for breakfast. Kyle dragged himself through the early day, resisting the urge to sample coffee again, regardless of how badly he wanted and needed the caffeine boost.

At noon, Mairi came over and they finally finished the science project. Kyle wanted to break into applause that the stupid thing was done. Over the past few days, he'd come to hate the project, to resent it for taking away time that could have been spent working on Ultitron. But he was careful not to let his animosity show to Mairi.

"Are you all right?" she asked him as she shrugged into her coat, ready to leave. "You look really tired."

Her concern gratified him and even perked him up a little. "I just had trouble sleeping last night. I'm fine."

Before leaving, Mairi did something she never did: She hugged Kyle. Perplexed, he didn't think to hug her back until it was too late and she had already pulled away. "Thanks for your help. I know this wasn't the project you wanted to work on originally, but you did a great job," Mairi said. Then she waved to him and left.

Kyle didn't know how to feel about that, especially since he knew that Mairi was going straight from his house to Mighty Mike's house, where she planned to have dinner with Mike and his foster parents. He idly wondered what the odds were of the same girl becoming friends with the two kids in town with superpowers. It seemed almost impossible for it to be a coincidence. What if it wasn't? What if Mike had some reason for being chummy with Mairi? That was a frightening thought: the idea of Mairi being in Mike's sights for some nefarious reason. He would pretend to be her friend and then do . . . Who knew what?

By the time the Mad Mask arrived for their nightly work session, Kyle wasn't tired anymore. The thought of Mairi in Mike's clutches had given him a second wind and he was once again downstairs, slaving over the obstinate motivational engine. No matter what he did, he just couldn't get it to work!

So absorbed was he in his task that he didn't even look up when the basement door opened and the Mad Mask entered.

"Good evening, Azure Avenger!"

"Hey, Mask."

"*Mad* Mask. *The* Mad Mask, preferably."

"Right."

"Frustration is evident in your voice, Azure Avenger. What troubles you, my friend?"

Kyle let out a sigh. He didn't want to admit it, but he had to: "I've been working on the motivational engine for days and I still can't get it to work."

The Mad Mask stroked the chin of his mask as if it were his own chin. "Interesting. Have you followed the schematics?"

"Exactly!" Kyle's frustration bubbled over and he threw down the screwdriver he'd been holding. "I followed them to the letter! They didn't make any sense to me, but I assembled it exactly the way you laid it out on the —"

"Then it must work. The plans are flawless." The Mad Mask spoke in a tone that left no room for disagreement.

Kyle disagreed anyway. "But —"

"Flawless," the Mad Mask repeated, and came over to stand behind Kyle. "Try it again."

Kyle rolled his eyes but went ahead and fiddled with

the control mechanism built into the motivational engine. To his utter shock, the engine lit up and the tiny servo-mechanisms deep inside began to rotate and shoot out the information lasers that would carry data to Ultitron's limbs.

"How . . ." Kyle's eyes bugged out at the fully functional motivational engine. "How . . . It didn't . . ."

"Again: The plans are flawless," the Mad Mask said smugly, and went to examine another component.

Kyle shook his head as if to wake himself up. What had changed? Had he not triggered the controls properly before? After a few minutes scrutinizing the schematics and the engine, he couldn't figure out what had gone wrong . . . or what had eventually gone right. The Mad Mask might be smug, but he totally deserved to be. Clearly his genius was leagues beyond Kyle's own. It surprised Kyle that he could think this without being angry or offended. Maybe if it hadn't been a friend, he would mind. But since the Mad Mask and he were allies, it didn't bother him the way it might have otherwise.

"Kyle," said the Mad Mask. It was the first time he had ever used Kyle's real name, and the sound of it in that deep, booming voice, echoing in behind the ebony mask, jolted Kyle.

"Yes?"

"During our hours together, you have explained your philosophy and your 'Prankster Manifesto.'" Kyle had rambled at length about the Manifesto and about his history of pranksterism. And the Mad Mask had actually been listening, it turned out. "The Mad Mask has given careful and due consideration to this doctrine and has concluded that it has merit."

"Oh? Really?"

"Watch the road carefully on your way to school tomorrow. You will be . . . amused. Of this, I have no doubt."

Kyle wondered what the heck *that* meant, but he knew better than to ask. The Mad Mask only doled out information on a need-to-know basis. He was like his own personal top secret spy agency. If Kyle didn't absolutely, positively need to know something, there was no way the Mad Mask was going to reveal it.

Still, Kyle was pleased that he'd made such an impression on the Mad Mask. Now that he thought about it, the Mad Mask was the first convert to the ideals of the Prankster Manifesto, and what a convert he was! A beyond-genius-level intellect had examined Kyle's personal ethos and agreed with it. Kyle couldn't keep from beaming.

"A thought," the Mad Mask said. He'd wandered over to the biochemical forge and struck his usual stance, hands clasped behind his back, standing stiffly upright. "This machinery has useful components. We should disassemble it."

At first, Kyle thought he must have misheard or mis-understood. "You want to cannibalize the biochemical forge?"

" 'Want' does not enter into the equation. We require certain components to finish Ultitron. Your 'biochemical forge' contains those components. Hence and therefore. And ergo."

Kyle gnawed at his bottom lip. What the Mad Mask said made perfect sense, but still — he just couldn't bring himself to do it. It had taken him weeks to assemble the biochemical forge. Originally, it was to be powered by the small nuclear reactor he'd built in the corner, but then he'd had to take apart the reactor in order to save the world from the ASE. So he'd found a way to power the forge with sunlight, and he was enormously proud of that innovation. And then there was the matter of the Axis theft, a daring broad-daylight heist of the necessary, rare chemical compounds. Even now, within the forge bubbled the chemical stew that would eventu-ally yield the bacteria that would rob Mighty Mike of his powers.

Taking Kyle's hesitation for outright mutiny, the Mad Mask fiercely stomped over to Kyle, towering over him. "Does your confidence waver, or merely your courage?" he jeered. "Speak now! Are you uncertain about your destiny, or merely afraid of it?"

Even backed up against the workbench, Kyle bristled

at the taunt. He was afraid of nothing and no one. "I'm just wondering . . . Isn't there another way to —"

"Do you think the Mad Mask would suggest a course of action without contemplating all possible, indeed all *conceivable*, alternatives? Do you? *Do you?*"

Kyle had to admit that was pretty unlikely.

Over the Mad Mask's shoulder, he could make out the control panel to the biochemical forge. Two steadily blinking lights told him that the internal processes were well within tolerances.

But if Ultitron was everything the Mad Mask promised . . .

(And Kyle had no reason to doubt that it would be.)

. . . if Ultitron was as powerful as the schematics made it seem . . .

(And why wouldn't it be, having been designed by the inventor of that amazing force field?)

. . . then what on earth did he even need the bacterium for? Ultitron would wipe up the ground with Mighty Mike, and when the alien pretender fled back to whatever planet he'd come from, it would prove to the world once and for all that its "hero" was nothing but a phony and that only Kyle (and the Mad Mask, of course) could be relied on to tell the truth and do what was right.

"Okay," he heard himself say. "Let's take it apart."

He handed a wrench to the Mad Mask, who stepped back without taking it. "It is your handiwork. You must dismantle it."

After a moment's hesitation, Kyle shut off the forge, drained the tank back into the barrel from Axis, and then began the process of stripping down the biochemical forge. The Mad Mask supervised, occasionally picking up and examining a part or piece, then setting it in a special pile.

In a soft voice, the Mad Mask said, "I admire your dedication." It was one of the few times he used the personal pronoun, so Kyle paid special attention. "Not everyone would discern the greater good to be had by destroying their own work for the betterment of mankind. You can and did. You are a rare individual, Kyle Camden."

Kyle's chest swelled with pride, but he didn't want to appear arrogant in front of the Mad Mask. "Well," he said humbly, "you can't make an omelet without breaking a few eggs." It was one of his father's more obvious clichés, but it suddenly seemed very appropriate.

"Omelets! The Mad Mask enjoys omelets!"

"Um, okay." Kyle struggled with a wrench and finally disconnected a hose from the intake valve in the forge.

"Especially with mushrooms and peppers. But only when the peppers are diced very finely."

"Got it."

Kyle worked late into the night, carefully dismantling his handiwork as the Mad Mask described his favorite omelet and then proceeded to hold forth on the best way to make hash browns.

The next day, an exhausted Kyle dragged himself to the bus stop. He'd considered trying to choke down the hot swill of coffee, but even as tired as he was, he couldn't visit that torture upon his taste buds once again. So instead he just asked Erasmus to play a subsonic alpha wave booster through his earbuds, a frequency designed to stimulate all the right parts of his brain. By the time his bus arrived, he was nearly awake.

"Did you notice the Mad Mask talking about Mairi last night?" Erasmus asked.

Kyle couldn't really talk back without arousing suspicion. He ducked low behind his seat and murmured, "He was talking about omelets."

"After that. I guess you were too focused on the forge to listen. He kept talking about Mairi and how beautiful she was."

"What?" Kyle wanted to say more, but the bus had stopped and the object of the Mad Mask's attention had just gotten on. Mairi made her way to the back of the bus and slid into the seat next to Kyle.

"Good morning!"

"Uh, hi."

"Are you okay?" Her brow furrowed with concern. "Why are you staring at me?"

Kyle blinked. "Oh. Nothing. Sorry." Beautiful? Mairi? Well, maybe. He'd never really thought of her that way before. She was just . . . Mairi. She wasn't beautiful; she wasn't ugly. She was just Mairi. Scrutinizing her now, he tried to see her the way the Mad Mask had seen her. That red hair, those green eyes that almost glowed . . .

"Kyle, you're still st —"

The screaming cut her off.

CHAPTER
TWELVE

In an instant, Kyle realized what was going on: the parking meters. The parking meters along Major Street, where the bus now trundled and shook its way to school.

The parking meters were exploding.

"*Watch the road carefully on your way to school tomorrow,*" the Mad Mask had said the night before. "*You will be . . . amused. Of this, I have no doubt.*"

Did he mean this? He couldn't! This wasn't amusing — this was dangerous!

Each parking meter was stuffed full of quarters from the early-morning commuters who parked along Major Street. As a meter exploded, quarters flew out in all directions, moving at such speed that they were like hot, deadly ninja throwing stars. As Kyle watched, a meter blew up and windows across the street shattered. Car alarms whined into the morning sky. Commuters and pedestrians dove for cover.

Another meter exploded and the school bus lurched as the tires on the right side deflated, punctured by blazing fast quarters.

An instant later, windows on that side of the bus started breaking, glass showering inward. Kids screamed and ducked as shards rained down over them.

Major Street became chaotic: Cars slammed to a halt, while other cars sped up. Traffic jammed and snarled. Horns blared. Alarms sang. People ran; people dived; people stood still in terror.

"What have you done?" Kyle whispered.

"I'm picking up a remote detonation signal," Erasmus reported. "I might be able to jam it by modifying my Wi-Fi band."

"Do it," Kyle said.

Mairi spun around to look at him, her eyes wide in fear. "Who are you *talking* to?"

"I said, 'Duck!'" Kyle said, and grabbed Mairi by the shoulders and pulled her down just as a large, jagged sheet of glass spun through the air where her head had been. It missed her by a whisker and smashed into Kyle's face. Kyle blinked at the impact and looked around to make sure no one had seen.

"Stay down," he told Mairi. The bus limped along on two good tires and two flats. The bus driver was yelling for kids to get down and stay calm, but it was tough to hear him over the panic. Kyle kept his hands on Mairi's shoulders, forcing her down as he furiously looked around for some way he could help.

There was no pattern to the explosions. Parking meters lined both sides of Major Street. Sometimes one from the north side would blow, sometimes one from the south. Sometimes two next to each other, sometimes two from different ends of the block. It was like being caught in an ambush, with a hundred insane gunmen all firing whenever they felt like it.

Kyle didn't want to reveal his powers to everyone on the bus, but he didn't think he had a choice. Someone could get really hurt —

Just then, the bus's brakes screeched so loud that the sound made Kyle's teeth vibrate. A car had slammed to a halt in the intersection in front of them, its windshield a spiderweb of fissures, and the bus driver had to hit the brakes to keep from colliding with it. But the bus was so unbalanced, its right side low on the deflated tires . . . Kyle could tell from the wobble of the bus, from its velocity and torque . . .

He did the calculations quickly in his head.

"We're gonna tip over," he said.

Sure enough, a moment later, the bus jackknifed and filled with the screams of kids as it pitched this way and that, finally tipping over onto the right side, the one with the two punctured tires.

There was a moment of shocked silence, and then everyone started screaming again. The bus was on its side, and all the kids who'd been sitting on the left side of the bus had collapsed and dropped onto the kids on the right side. Moans and groans filled the air.

Fortunately, Kyle had seen this coming. Even though he was sitting on the left side, he'd managed to brace himself between the wall and the seat back, then looped an arm through Mairi's backpack so that she was hanging from it instead of dropping like everyone else had. She looked up at him in confusion and gratitude and fear, and in that moment Kyle thought that maybe he saw what the Mad Mask saw. Maybe Mairi was beautiful.

"Gonna let you down now," he told her, pretending to be straining with the effort of holding her up.

"Be careful," she said. "Don't hurt yourself."

Kyle had to laugh in the privacy of his own head. He could pick up the entire bus and not feel it.

He lowered Mairi safely to the "floor," what had once been the right-hand side of the bus, then joined her there.

"We have to get out of here," Mairi said.

"No," Kyle told her. "This is the safest place right now." The roof of the bus was just ahead of him — he reached out and rapped it with his knuckles. "This is good-old-fashioned steel. Best protection against what's going on out there." Kyle glanced over to the front of the bus — the driver was slumped in his seat, dangling from his seat belt, unconscious.

"See if you can get everyone organized and have them gather in toward the front, against the roof, okay?" Kyle headed for the emergency door.

"Where are *you* going?" she demanded.

"Outside. To, uh, see what's happening."

Mairi leveled a gaze at him for a moment, then relented. "Just be careful, okay? You're not Mighty Mike, you know."

He grinned at her and gave a thumbs-up. "I don't have to be."

Mairi crawled along the seat backs to the center of the bus, gathering kids and urging them all to the front. Kyle checked the emergency door. It had been crumpled shut by the crash. He applied a little strength to it and forced it open with a grating whine.

"I think I've blocked the Wi-Fi signal," Erasmus reported.

"Good. I have to check out the damage."

He crawled out of the bus into madness. Major Street had become a war zone. Cars had bumped up on the sidewalks, slammed into fire hydrants, collided with each other. Drivers sat collapsed behind the wheel or staggered around the street in a daze. The smart people had hit the ground, curled into protective fetal positions or lying prone with their hands over their heads.

Up the street, a parking meter exploded.

"Oops. Missed one," Erasmus said.

Kyle hesitated for a moment. Just a moment. He could rush to intercept the quarters before they caused further havoc, but people would see, people would know —

"Oh, thank God!" someone called, and Kyle didn't even need to look to see that Mighty Mike had arrived.

"What took you so long?" he mumbled, and retreated back into the bus.

It was an hour before the police signaled that Major Street was clear and safe for people to emerge from their hiding places. Ambulances lined the street now, and the entire Bouring Police Department had arrived for crowd control. Kyle cynically thought that this would be the perfect time for someone to pull a crime somewhere else in town. He filed the information away for the future — create a big enough disturbance and you could get every cop in Bouring to abandon their posts.

Fortunately, no one had been killed. There were plenty of injuries, some of them serious, but from the chatter Erasmus was picking up on the police band, it had been a lucky day for everyone involved.

Kyle stood with the rest of the kids from the bus in a line near one of the ambulances. His parents — like every other parent in Bouring — had rushed to Major Street in a panic as soon as they heard what happened. They stood on the other side of a police barricade, and Kyle waved to them to show that he was fine. Everyone caught in the crossfire had to be checked out by paramedics, then either sent to the hospital or released to go home.

Mighty Mike, of course, had set things to rights as soon as he'd arrived on the scene. He had decapitated the remaining parking meters and tossed them sky-high. Kyle wondered where they had landed — he didn't really trust Mike enough to assume that the kid was smart enough to hurl them somewhere safe.

But in the meantime, Mike had managed to stop four more car collisions, rescue people trapped under fallen debris, and generally do all of the things you'd expect a hero to do in this situation. He even made sure the paramedics came first to a pregnant woman who'd gone into labor with the shock of the explosions. (The baby was fine, and the woman swore she would name her new daughter "Mike.") It was pretty much the only time Kyle had seen Mike in action and *not* seen him make some sort of mistake. As long as those discarded parking meter heads hadn't landed anywhere dangerous, Kyle had to grudgingly give Mike a passing grade. This time.

Now Mike lingered, hovering over the scene, arms

folded over his chest, watching. Kyle didn't like having him floating overhead. Like he was somehow surveilling everything and everyone. It made him shiver.

As Kyle waited in line, Sheriff Monroe strode over to him. "Camden! I wanna talk to you."

Kyle gritted his teeth. "I'm a little busy," he said.

"Waiting in line? I don't think so." The sheriff grabbed Kyle's arm and pulled him out of line.

"Hey!"

"We need to talk. You and me." Monroe leaned in close, his dirty yellow mustache quivering. "This time you've gone too far. People could have been killed. You hear me? You think that makes your point? You think that's funny?"

Kyle jerked his arm back. "Are you nuts? I didn't do this! I was on the bus when it happened!"

Mairi stepped out of line and stomped over to the sheriff. "Sheriff Monroe! Kyle did *not* do this! He was with me in the bus and he kept me from getting hurt." She stamped her foot for emphasis and glared with her piercing green eyes.

Monroe's lips quirked. He looked like he was about to say something, but just then a shadow fell over him and a soft voice from above said, "Can I be of assurance, Sheriff?"

They all looked up to see Mighty Mike, arms still crossed over his chest.

"You mean 'assistance,'" Mairi said helpfully. "And I think everything's under control. Isn't it, Sheriff?"

Monroe squinted at Kyle, who tried to look as innocent as possible. He'd had nothing to do with this insanity, but he knew who did, and he didn't want Monroe to pick up on that.

"We're done for now, Camden." He stalked away.

Mighty Mike landed between Kyle and Mairi. "Are you KO'd, Kyle?"

"I'm fine," Kyle said, ignoring his goof.

"And Mairi." Mike turned to Mairi and took her hands in his own. "I was so worried you might be mingled in the disaster."

"That's 'mangled,'" Kyle informed him.

"Kyle kept me from getting hurt," Mairi said. "Don't worry about me. There are other people who need your help."

Mighty Mike nodded curtly. He turned to Kyle and smiled. "Thanks for your help."

"Sure thing," Kyle said, hatred seething inside him.

Mighty Mike took off. Mairi and Kyle stared at each other.

"Kyle, what happened here?" Mairi asked. "Is this what it's going to be like now? Is the Blue Freak always going to be attacking the town?"

Kyle opened his mouth to say that it wasn't the Blue Freak, but realized that there was no way he could know that for sure, unless he was the Blue Freak. And he couldn't tell Mairi that.

Instead, he just shrugged his shoulders and then the two of them got back in line.

Kyle paced impatiently as he waited for the Mad Mask in the basement that night. As soon as the door opened, Kyle started in on him, yelling in the loudest whisper he dared to use.

"Are you insane?" he demanded. "Have you completely lost your mind? People could have been killed today! Your little stunt today could have —"

The Mad Mask drew himself up to his full height. "The Mad Mask will not be spoken to thusly! Comport yourself with respect and dignity!"

He didn't say "or else." He didn't have to. His posture and the memory of that powerful force field were enough to make Kyle take a step back and draw in a deep breath.

"Look," he said, "what you did today was really dangerous. I almost had to reveal my identity. Do you get it?"

The Mad Mask tilted his head. "I merely attempted to place your 'Prankster Manifesto' into greater context."

"No. You . . . you executed a terrorist attack on a town! That's not a prank."

The Mad Mask snorted hollowly in his mask. "Your Manifesto's stated goal is to elucidate people's own innate absurdity. To wit, showing them not to take themselves so seriously. Showing them their own foolish natures. My prank did this. It forced people to confront what is truly serious and meaningful — their own lives. It compelled them to put aside the silly notions of the workaday world and focus on the core matter of living. As such, it is a highly successful prank."

"You've got it all twisted up!" Kyle protested. He held up a sheet of paper on which he'd written the Prankster Manifesto:

THE PRANKSTER MANIFESTO
BY KYLE CAMDEN

1. PEOPLE ARE FOOLISH.
2. SERIOUS PEOPLE ARE DOUBLY FOOLISH. ESPECIALLY PEOPLE IN AUTHORITY: PARENTS, TEACHERS, ETC.
3. PRANKS SHOW PEOPLE HOW FOOLISH THEY ARE.
4. IT'S GOOD TO SHOW PEOPLE HOW FOOLISH THEY ARE BECAUSE THEN THEY STOP ACTING SO SERIOUS.
5. WHEN THEY STOP ACTING SO SERIOUS, THEY CAN UNDERSTAND THE TRUTH.
6. WHICH IS THAT THEY'RE FOOLISH.
7. KYLE CAMDEN IS ALLOWED TO BE SERIOUS BECAUSE HE'S NOT FOOLISH.

"You made people *more* serious!" Kyle told him. "And besides, a prank is supposed to be *funny*."

"I found it quite amusing to watch the denizens of Bouring running hither and yon, looking for shelter from an attack that was as nonsensical as it was unexpected."

"You've got a weird sense of humor," Kyle muttered.

The Mad Mask shrugged. It was the most humble, most normal thing Kyle had ever seen the Mad Mask do. "Do not attempt to understand the mind of the Mad Mask."

"Maybe from now on, I should stick to the pranks and you should stick to the . . . to the . . . giant robot building and teleporting and force fielding."

Again the Mad Mask shrugged, as if to say, *Makes no difference to me.*

"Just one thing," Kyle said. "You need to understand this: Pranking is about showing people they're stupid. It's not about hurting people. There's no point to hurting people."

The Mad Mask stood silent for a long moment and then, in a voice chillingly cold, said, "The world must feel the pain the Mad Mask feels."

from the top secret journal of
Kyle Camden (deciphered):

I have to admit today made me nervous about working with the Mad Mask. Anyone who could wreak the kind of havoc he wreaked on Major Street . . . That's just crazy.

I spent most of the day trying to decide what to do. A part of me wanted to attack him as soon as he came into the basement, but I realized that would be no good. With that force field, he's strictly a hands-off kind of guy. There's no way I can stop him.

The more I thought about it, the more I realized that talking to him was the only way to go. Fortunately for me, it was also the best way.

I think basically he just didn't get the Prankster Manifesto. It's very clear to me because 1) I created it, and 2) I've had a lot of time to think about it. But the Mad Mask approaches it from a genius perspective. He cut straight to the core — make people realize how foolish they are, make them less serious — and he decided that the quickest way to do that was to put people in fear for their lives.

In a way, it's elegant in its simplicity. It's sort of like Alexander the Great and the Gordian knot. The Gordian knot was this big, complicated knot that no one could untie. People spent years trying to figure it out, and then Alexander came along and just cut the thing in half with his sword. Ta-da! Problem solved, right?

Alexander went on to rule most of the world of his time and became one of the most famous figures in history.

That's sort of how the Mad Mask thinks, I guess.

He just forgot that a prank needs to be clever. It needs to be funny. It needs to make people think. Not think as in, "Oh, my God, I'm about to die!" but as in, "Oh, gee, I sure do act stupid most of the time; how can I change that?"

We spent some time talking about it and I think he gets it now. Now that we're focused on Ultitron again, things are back to normal. The Mad Mask has chilled out about his very poorly thought-out "prank." I don't think he'll try anything like that again.

Once we had all of the pranking issues straightened out, we were able to get back to work on Ultitron. We made a lot of progress! In fact, we have the motivational engine ready to be connected, and all of the subsystems are working and online. The Mad Mask says we only need one more specialized component . . . and that we can't build that one. We're going to have to steal it.

I'm fine with this. It's just one more thing, after all. We steal this last little piece of gadgetry, we install it in Ultitron, and then everything will be fine. Ultitron will wipe out Mighty Mike and then the world will finally see the truth: Mike the pretender, the alien. And the Azure Avenger ready to guide the world into a new age of perfection.

If I have to commit some little crime to get there, what's the big deal, right? I just have to stay focused on what matters: exposing Mighty Mike. If he is really the good guy everyone thinks he is, then why hasn't he told the world he's an alien? Why hasn't he revealed his true purpose on Earth? I don't like the idea of him being here and not owning up to who and what he is. So whatever I have to do . . . I'll do.

Erasmus, though, is not happy. About anything at all.

He's still obsessed with the Mad Mask's attempt at a "prank" earlier today. "He's dangerous, Kyle. How can you trust someone who thinks like that?"

I tried to explain that the Mad Mask just made a mistake. That he didn't really understand the Prankster Manifesto. Maybe there's even a teeny, tiny chance that I could have explained it a little bit better. I've been so tired lately that maybe — maybe! — I gave the wrong impression.

Plus, Erasmus couldn't see the Mad Mask when we were talking. Erasmus is a great artificial intelligence, but he doesn't have eyes — he couldn't see the slump in the Mad Mask's shoulders or his posture or anything like that when I was explaining where he went wrong with the parking meter prank.

I mean, "prank."

Erasmus doesn't want to hear anything like that. He keeps swearing that the Mad Mask is bad news. So I had to make a decision.

I didn't want to switch off Erasmus or remove his power supply, but he was nagging an awful lot. So finally I came up with a compromise: I hooked him up to the brain-wave manipulator and told him to fix it.

"What do you mean?" he demanded.

"The side effects are getting ridiculous. Mom's twitching like she's possessed and Dad can't stop stuttering. See what you can do about fixing that."

"But —"

I removed my earbuds and that was that.

Time for bed. Tomorrow's a busy day.

CHAPTER
THIRTEEN

The next day, after school, Kyle and the Mad Mask went to commit their final crime.

It was strange for Kyle to fly during the day and especially without Erasmus at his side and chattering in his ears. He sort of missed the electronic pain in his butt.

The Mad Mask had told Kyle that they would meet on the highway just across from Lundergaard Research (slogan: "We gaard more than just lunders!"), a local think tank and technology firm with mostly military contracts. "Within the bowels of Lundergaard Research," the Mad Mask had intoned, "we shall find the final component that shall bring the mighty Ultitron to life!"

Sounded good to Kyle.

He flew high so that no one could see him. Soon enough, he saw the massive spread of the Lundergaard facility below him. It was like a school campus, more than a dozen interlinked buildings sprawling over what had once been acres of soybean fields. Kyle supposed that it was a blight on the natural beauty of the area, but he didn't really care for soybeans, so it was no big deal.

"I'd rather have technology than soybeans," he said out loud.

Usually, Erasmus would have chimed in with some snarky fact about soybeans. Kyle sighed into his mask and scanned the area across the highway from Lundergaard for the Mad Mask. A flashing bright light nearly blinded him — the Mad Mask's signal. Kyle blinked to clear his vision, then darted downward as quickly as he could, hoping no one would spot him.

Among some bushes and trees, the Mad Mask stood tall and confident, a tiny mirror in one hand. That's how he had signaled to Kyle: reflecting sunlight back into the sky.

"Welcome, Azure Avenger! Are you ready for the penultimate step in the birthing of the glorious Ultitron?"

Kyle's pulse pounded just a bit harder and faster at the question. He *was* ready. Ultitron was the Mad Mask's "baby," not Kyle's, but in the past week or so, Kyle had come to think of the gigantic robot as just as much his project, too. Now — soon — Ultitron would come to life. And the world would never be the same.

"I'm ready," Kyle said. "Look, while I was flying overhead, I, you know . . ." He unsnapped one of the pouches on his belt, took out a pair of high-powered binoculars, and gestured with them. "I checked out Lundergaard from above. Their security is —"

"Pah!" The Mad Mask waved a dismissive hand. "Bother me not with such things! The Mad Mask knows of their security, having hacked into a military satellite weeks ago to observe them. Their security forces cannot withstand the combined might of the Mad Mask and the Azure Avenger!"

"Well, maybe not, but still —"

"We go now!" the Mad Mask crowed, pointing across the highway. "We march . . . into history!"

Who could argue with that? Not Kyle. "Let's go!" he shouted.

A moment later, as they pressed through brambles to the highway, he thought to ask, "Um, how are we going to get in?"

He couldn't see it, of course, but Kyle imagined that the Mad Mask smiled.

Quite unbelievably, they walked up to the front gate.

Kyle was nervous as they strode across the highway together and approached it. The gate was a huge, twelve-foot-high affair made of steel that stood between thick concrete walls that ringed the entire Lundergaard complex. Kyle knew from his flyover that the concrete walls were more than five feet thick. A sign hanging on the gate said:

LUNDERGAARD RESEARCH AND TECHNOLOGIES
THIS FACILITY IS FOR AUTHORIZED PERSONNEL ONLY!
ARMY CODE USC J-783681-1951 APPLIES!
NO PHOTOGRAPHY PERMITTED

A guard stood at attention near a control panel built into the wall. He looked bored, but he perked up as Kyle and the Mad Mask approached. He had a very serious-looking rifle slung over one arm, and while he didn't point it at them, he kept one hand on it.

"Halloween isn't for another week, kids," he said. "And we don't give out candy anyway."

"Open the gate," the Mad Mask said in utter seriousness.

The guard chuckled, but Kyle detected a bit of nervousness under the laughter. "No treats, so you're pulling a trick? I'm telling you, kids, you — Hey, wait." His eyes narrowed and he looked at Kyle. "Are you actually dressed as the Blue —"

"Open the gate," the Mad Mask insisted, "and your life will be spared when the mighty Ultitron comes."

The guard realized now that something was wrong. This wasn't just two kids messing around. He raised his rifle with one hand and felt behind him for the control panel with the other.

The Mad Mask lifted his hand and the guard fired! Kyle shouted out as the crack of the rifle filled the air. At the same moment, laser-chaff exploded from the Mad Mask's gauntlet, blinding the guard and sending him spinning to collide with the concrete wall and then collapse to the ground, clawing at his blinded eyes.

"Are you okay?" Kyle asked, checking the Mad Mask for injuries. But of course the force field had protected him.

"The Mad Mask is unharmed. Tear down the gate, Azure Avenger."

"Why don't we just fly over it? Or teleport through?"

"The Mad Mask wants the world to know we have arrived! No more questions! Tear down this gate!"

It didn't make much sense to Kyle. Teleporting or flying would be much easier, and people would still know eventually. But there was no time for questions. He grabbed two of the upright steel bars in his hands and took a deep breath. The gate was massive and heavy, grounded and pegged in the thick concrete walls. He strained and pulled, starting slow at first because he didn't want to just rip out the bars. He had to rip down the entire gate.

"Quickly . . ." the Mad Mask murmured.

Kyle increased the pressure. Vibrating along the steel bars, he felt something deep within the gate give and break loose. He tugged with all his might, and the gate shrieked and complained and twisted free from its moorings, chunks of concrete collapsing into dust all around.

Alarms screamed.

For a moment, Kyle lost track of the Mad Mask in the chaos.

The alarm had gone off just as a cloud of choking concrete dust had whirled up and around. Kyle had tossed the mangled gate to one side, opening Lundergaard's campus to himself and the Mad Mask.

And then the attack started.

He didn't know where the first volley came from, but suddenly Kyle was assaulted on all sides. There were smoke grenades coming from every direction, as well as what were called "flash bangs" — special grenades that exploded in light and sound to distract and incapacitate. They were sort of an inferior, primitive version of Kyle's laser-chaff.

But Kyle had those glare-reducing lenses in his mask, so the flashes didn't bother him, and the Mad Mask had given both of them special earplugs that used white-sound circuitry to block the noises.

That smoke was annoying, though. Kyle spun around in a tight circle with both arms extended, whirling faster and faster until the smoke got caught up in the mini-twister he'd created and began funneling up into the sky.

Which revealed dozens of armed guards pouring out of the Lundergaard buildings, all of them rushing toward Kyle.

Wow.

Kyle stopped spinning and stumbled a little bit. Head rush!

From the left, a water cannon blasted Kyle at top pressure. From the right, a platoon of guards fired an electrified net.

Oh, these people were just too stupid!

Kyle ducked under the net and let it hit the water. The net shorted out, but not before an electrical jolt surged back along the water blast and blew up the cannon.

Mass panic now. People running everywhere. Kyle knew that it was only a matter of time before the guards brought out the real ammo, the live stuff that could kill people. He was pretty sure that none of it could hurt him, but he didn't want bullets bouncing off his body and drilling through innocent guards. Just because these guys got a paycheck from Lundergaard didn't mean they deserved to die.

He looked around for the Mad Mask. Even though it was anarchy all around him, the special earplugs made everything eerily quiet.

The Mad Mask stood off to one side, near a big SUV.

All sorts of rubber bullets were bouncing off his force field and he seemed not to notice that he was in the middle of a massive firefight. Instead, he just stood there with his hands clasped behind his back, gazing up at the sky.

A guard came close to Kyle and swung at him with the butt of his rifle. Kyle easily ducked, grabbed the rifle, and jerked it out of the guard's hands. There was something delicious and thrilling about seeing the look of absolute terror on the face of a full-grown man.

Kyle twisted the rifle into a pretzel shape and tossed it to the guard, who reflexively caught it, still staring in fear. Kyle laughed, then darted forward and flicked the man's jaw with a fraction of his strength. The guard went flying through the air and crumpled to the ground, unconscious.

Just then, the guards started pointing up. Kyle knew what he would see even before he followed their fingers.

Mighty Mike.

Before Mike could land, Kyle sped to the Mad Mask's side. "I'll hold him off," Kyle shouted, hoping the Mad Mask could hear him through the special earplugs. "You get inside and find the stuff we need!"

If the Mad Mask heard, he didn't acknowledge it, standing still as Kyle launched himself into the air to intercept Mighty Mike. Mike's mouth was moving, but

Kyle couldn't hear what he was saying, which was just as well — it was probably stupid.

He didn't give Mike a chance to attack first; Kyle knew from experience that Mighty Mike would throw a punch without provocation, so he decided to be proactive and launched a hook at Mike's face.

Mike blocked the blow, but only barely. Kyle followed up with a right cross before Mike could react, nailing Mike in the side of the head. Mike spun around in midair, spraying spittle. Kyle's heart jumped a little in joy. He normally despised physical violence — and was usually worried that in a fight Mike might rip his mask off — but right now, he was happy to make an exception. He kept pummeling Mike, not letting up, not letting Mike catch his breath, until a final massive blow sent Mike spiraling back twenty yards through the air.

With a little breathing room, Kyle glanced over his shoulder quickly to check on the Mad Mask's progress, but he didn't see his ally anywhere near the Lundergaard buildings. Where *was* the Mad Mask . . . ?

And then he realized that all of the guards had concentrated their efforts on an SUV that was barreling toward the gate, hauling butt to the exit.

Wait. Not just *an* SUV. It was the same SUV the Mad Mask had been standing near.

Kyle had two thoughts pop into his head at once: The first one was *Wow, the Mad Mask is driving without his license!* and the second one was *Where's he going?* He tossed the first one aside (they were breaking into a government-related research facility; a little something like underage driving was no big deal) and focused on the second. The Mad Mask hadn't even had time to go into the building, much less find and grab the missing component! Why was he running away already?

Was he scared? No. Impossible. What the heck was going —?

Just then, Kyle heard the sound of gunfire from below, the shouts of the guards running to and fro, the revving of the SUV engine as the vehicle bounced through the gate and jerked crazily onto the highway.

He also heard wind. Mighty Mike, soaring in.

He *heard* . . .

His earplugs had stopped working!

Kyle barely had time to turn around when Mike plowed into him from behind. Kyle screamed in shock and pain as Mike tackled him like a linebacker taking down a quarterback. He flipped over himself, a backward aerial somersault that carried him into a tall Lundergaard building. The wall crumbled around him and he kept going; concrete, glass, and steel shattered and he finally collapsed on an office floor somewhere inside.

As disorienting as being knocked through a wall was, he was even more knocked off balance by the Mad

Mask's sudden turn. What had happened? Why had the Mad Mask fled? What was he supposed to do now?

Mighty Mike burst into the office, threading the hole Kyle had made when he'd crashed in. "Okay, Blue Freak — time for you to settle your bat!"

Kyle winced as he got to his feet. They circled each other like boxers, wary. "I think you mean settle my '*tab*.'"

"Whatever."

"Alien freak!" Kyle clenched his fists.

"Joking jokester!"

"What?"

"It sounded good to me!" Mike said defensively.

"Are we gonna fight or not?"

"Tell me where your partner went and I'll go easy on you," Mike said.

"Never!" Kyle spat.

It was easy to be so defiant when he had absolutely no idea where the Mad Mask was going. Or why.

The Mad Mask drove at two miles below the speed limit, not wanting to attract any police attention. He knew some of the Lundergaard guards had seen him leave in the SUV, but he figured that they would be more than occupied by the battle between the Azure Avenger and Mighty Mike.

He grinned under his mask. Mighty Mike had, of course, shown up. The Mad Mask had been certain that the do-gooder child would show up at Lundergaard at precisely the right moment, but just to be sure, the Mad Mask had sent a distress call to the Bouring Police Department, guaranteeing that Mighty Mike would end up at Lundergaard.

It was, the Mad Mask thought, too bad that the Azure Avenger would have to be sacrificed. In the past few days, the Mad Mask had come to enjoy his time with Kyle, especially the youngster's quick mind. But the Mad Mask had a cause, a sacred mission, and nothing could stand in its way.

The parking meters had been a test, a test that Kyle had failed beyond belief. The boy claimed to want to educate the world, but when push came to shove, he did not have the spine — the steel — to do what must be done. The Mad Mask had always thought that the Azure Avenger would make a good patsy for his own crimes. The "Blue Freak" was known to the world — he could have been the face of the Mad Mask's reign of terror.

The Mad Mask was going to destroy beauty. He was going to make the world feel the pain he felt. There was no room for sympathy or compassion in his plan, and Kyle had proven an unfit partner. Ultitron must stride the world like a god, with no one and nothing to stop him. Certainly not misguided, misplaced sentiment for the mere mortals in his path, the puling weaklings destined and fit only to be crushed beneath his tread!

The Mad Mask laughed, a loud, sustained manic belly laugh. He pulled onto the off-ramp for Bouring, driving past the sign that read YOU ARE ABOUT TO ENTER THE TOWN OF BOURING — IT'S NOT BORING! He needed to recover the motivational engine from Kyle's basement and then repair to his hidden lair, where he would install it. There was no "missing component" to be purloined from Lundergaard Research — that was merely a ruse to distract Mighty Mike and slough off the Azure Avenger. The Mad Mask wondered idly if the Azure Avenger would even survive the day; he seemed quite powerful but between Mighty Mike and the experimental weapons in storage at Lundergaard . . . Well, it seemed quite possible — likely, even — that the Azure Avenger would not live to see Ultitron's rampage and the Mad Mask's ultimate triumph over beauty itself!

Oh, well.

He braked to a halt in front of Kyle's house, no longer caring about concealing Kyle's secret identity. It was late in the afternoon, and the street was empty — kids were inside and parents weren't home from work yet. The Mad Mask strode up the walkway and kicked the front door. It held, and a shiver of pain ran up his leg to his groin. And yet, he did not cry out or otherwise acknowledge the pain. Pain was for lesser beings, not for the likes of the Mad Mask.

He kicked again. This time, the door jerked with the force of the blow, the lock breaking. Excellent!

"Hey!" a voice called out. "What are you doing?"

The Mad Mask turned around. There, behind him, stood the girl, the one the Azure Avenger called a friend. Mairi — that was her name.

Mairi gasped when the Mad Mask stood before her in all his glory. She took a step back.

Under his mask, the Mad Mask grinned a slow, evil grin.

"Hello, my dear," he said in a menacing tone. "Such a pleasure to see you again. And yes, now that I see you in the daylight, I can tell that you are quite . . . beautiful."

Mairi hardly had time to scream.

CHAPTER
FOURTEEN

At Lundergaard Research, what had once been called "Building 12" was now nothing more than rubble. Building 13 wasn't looking all that great, either. The Lundergaard security team had shifted its focus from repelling the attack on its facility to just doing its best to evacuate the entire campus without anyone getting killed. So far, they were doing a good job. But the sounds from Building 13 weren't encouraging: crashes, metallic shrieks, occasional explosions. Building 12 had made similar sounds just before it collapsed.

And now the superpowered kids were in Building 13 and showed no signs of stopping.

Somewhere deep inside Building 13, Kyle lashed out with what felt like his millionth punch. He was exhausted. Mighty Mike just would not give up. The two of them squared off against each other in what had once been a conference room but now was more like an example of what happens to a conference room when a family of tornadoes decides to move into the neighborhood.

"I'm telling you," Kyle said again, "you have to let me go. Something's happening —"

"Are you peanuts?" Mike said, absorbing the blow and kicking Kyle in the stomach. Kyle had gotten tired of correcting Mike's malapropisms and didn't even bother anymore. "I'm not letting you go! Look at all the damage you've caused."

"I've caused?" Kyle rubbed his belly, stepping back. "You're the one who punched me into the building in the first place!"

"I'm not arguing who's right with you!" Mike fumed. "Just surrender and this'll all be over!"

"Not a chance." Kyle ducked as black lasers stabbed at him from Mighty Mike's eyes. The wall behind him sizzled and hissed as it slowly melted away. "You're going to knock down this building, too!"

"I didn't knock down the other one!" Mike protested.

"You ripped up a support beam!"

"It wasn't *labeled*!"

Kyle rolled his eyes, which was a mistake because Mike plowed into him at top speed, and the two of them careened through the half-melted wall, blew through an office, and ended up smashing into a massive cubicle farm. They rolled on the floor, Mighty Mike on top, pummeling Kyle over and over.

"I need to *think*!" Kyle screamed, and lashed out with both feet. Ah! A good, solid connection — he caught Mike in the gut and tossed the punk off him . . . and through the ceiling.

What is going on here?

Kyle was no idiot: He figured that the Mad Mask had double-crossed him, using him to distract Mighty Mike while he escaped. But why? What was he up to —?

Just then, the phone rang.

Actually, *all* the phones rang.

Standing in shock in the midst of a hundred ringing phones, Kyle couldn't move for a second. Had he and Mike somehow damaged the phone system during their fight . . . and made all the phones go off? That wasn't likely.

Above, he heard sounds of crashing and thrashing as Mike fought his way clear of pieces of roof. He only had a few moments, and the phones kept ringing.

He grabbed the one on the nearest desk. "Um, hello?"

"Kyle!" It was Kyle's own voice, though broken up with static. Erasmus! "We've got problems."

"Little busy here." He almost asked how Erasmus had called him here, but he knew the answer because it was what he would have done in the same situation: Erasmus must have been wirelessly monitoring the news. The situation at Lundergaard would have been broadcast, so then Erasmus simply remotely hacked into Lundergaard's telephone system and commandeered the phones.

"No, a big problem," Erasmus went on. "The Mad Mask —"

"Betrayed me. I know!" He looked up. Mike would come through the hole in the ceiling any second now. . . .

"Listen to me! It's worse than that. He's been here."

The motivational engine! Kyle thought. Of course. Now it made sense. . . .

"And he took Mairi."

"He *what?*" Kyle turned away from the ceiling and slammed an angry fist into the desk, which — predictably — split in two, dumping its contents to the floor. A small porcelain pot broke open, spilling soil and a tiny ficus. Oops. For some reason, Kyle felt worse about that than knocking down that other building. Probably because knocking down the building was Mike's fault.

"It gets worse," Erasmus went on.

"Worse? How could —"

BOOM! Mighty Mike soared back into the room, pieces of acoustic ceiling tile and shredded electric cable streaming off him like water off a surfer. Kyle dropped the phone and dodged left, then right, then grabbed Mike's cape and spun him around in a circle.

Once. Twice. He let go and watched Mike go flailing through a wall.

This nonsense was getting Kyle nowhere. He needed a clear, quiet minute to figure out what was going on here. A minute without Mike trying to bash his brains in.

So he flew straight up, through the hole in the ceiling, then through the hole in the next ceiling, and so on until he found an intact ceiling (he'd kicked Mike through four stories — nice!) and crashed his way through that ceiling and the next until he finally burst through the roof of Building 13 into the open air. He figured he had thirty seconds before Mike followed him up here, so he had to use it. What could the Mad Mask be up to? And why had he kidnapped Mairi? And —

Oh, boy.

Off to the west, Kyle could see Bouring. Well, actually, he couldn't really see Bouring because Bouring was small and flat and no big deal. But he *could* see the Bouring Lighthouse, which stood up along the horizon, as obvious as a basketball player at a dwarves' convention.

And close by the lighthouse, like, say, the basketball player's twin brother, was Ultitron.

Kyle blinked. It was definitely Ultitron. It looked like a ten-story-tall replica of the Mad Mask, right down to a black-as-night face mask with a white tear-shaped blemish. He had spent so many hours poring over the schematics that he couldn't not recognize the robot for real. He had always known that Ultitron would be gigantic, but seeing it in real life, towering over the trees, was another thing entirely. It was awe-inspiring. A thrill of pride ran through Kyle — he had helped build it!

Yeah, and then the guy you helped betrayed you. . . .

Ultitron lurched a bit but made its way steadily toward the lighthouse. Kyle remembered how the Mad Mask had called the lighthouse beautiful. . . .

I thought it was a compliment. I'm an idiot! He hates *beauty. He's going to destroy the lighthouse! Mairi's mom's whole life is in there!*

And what about Mairi herself? What had the Mad Mask done with her? Or to her?

Just then, Mike exploded up through the rooftop, blowing out a new hole as he did so.

"You could have just used mine," Kyle said wearily.

Mike paused for a moment, glancing down as if realizing that, yes, he'd just caused more property damage than necessary.

Kyle snapped his fingers. "Hey, look!" he said. "Big robot! Fetch, boy!" He pointed.

Mike looked. For the first time ever, he actually seemed scared. For just a moment. Then he grimaced and set his jaw. "Just because I'm going to stop that robot doesn't mean I'm through with —"

"Right, right. Gotta go. Bye."

Kyle sped off. Checking over his shoulder, he watched as Mike sped off, too, at a different heading, bulleting straight for Ultitron. He knew Mike wouldn't let Ultitron go too far. And in the meantime, he had to figure out what had happened to Mairi. For that, he needed Erasmus.

Within seconds, he was home. It was getting dark out now, so no one saw him approach his house from the back, the side that faced the woods. He had started leaving his window unlocked, so it was easy to open and then glide into his room.

As he did so, he caught a glimpse of himself reflected in one of the giant TV screens. His costume was torn from being thrown around by Mighty Mike, big rips up and down his arms and torso, his cape in tatters. Fortunately, his mask was still intact. Through the holes in the fabric, he could see bruises forming. Yeah, he was invulnerable, but not to someone just as strong or stronger.

He checked on Lefty quickly — he remembered the Mad Mask saying something about eating Lefty. But his pet rabbit was fine, snoozing in his cage as though nothing had happened.

So Kyle snatched up Erasmus from the desk, took out the Mad Mask's now-useless earplugs, and slipped in his earbuds.

"Talk, Erasmus. You said things were worse than just kidnapping Mairi. How can they be worse than that?"

"He also took the brain-wave manipulator."

Kyle's heart froze in his chest. "Oh, God. My parents —"

"They weren't home from work yet. But, Kyle, here's the thing —"

"Talk on the way." Kyle flew out the window, arched his back, and shot straight into the sky.

"On the way? Where are we going?"

"Ultitron's on the loose. I figure when I tear into that thing like a chain saw opening a can of soup, the Mad Mask will surrender Mairi." He flipped around and flew north, using cloud cover to conceal his arrival.

"Kyle, you have to listen to me. About the brain-wave manipulator —"

"As long as he's not around my parents, it's fine."

"Listen! I fixed it! It'll work on anyone now. And the Mad Mask has it."

Kyle paused, hovering in midair. "You *fixed* it?"

"That's what you told me to do!"

"But now . . . He has the brain-wave manipulator. *And* he has Mairi!" Kyle shuddered. He didn't want to imagine what the Mad Mask could do to Mairi with the brain-wave manipulator at his disposal, but his imagination surged forward and painted a series of vivid pictures anyway: Mairi, brainwashed into becoming the Mad

Mask's sidekick. Mairi, her mind erased . . . Everything that made her unique and special and Kyle's only real friend, evaporated like dew under the hot morning sun.

"You can't just go blasting in there and take on Ultitron," Erasmus pleaded. "You have to think."

Erasmus was right. Of course he was right: He was based on Kyle's own thought patterns. And right now he was telling Kyle exactly what he needed to hear.

"Okay." He took a long, deep breath. It made him feel a little better. "What do we know?"

"According to the police band, Mighty Mike is keeping Ultitron from knocking down the lighthouse. But it's not easy."

At least Mike had his uses.

"What else do we know?" This is why he'd created Erasmus — talking out loud helped his thinking.

"Earlier today, I researched the Mad Mask."

"How did you do that?"

"I conducted a web search of missing fourteen-year-olds from nearby towns, cross-referenced to the dates shortly after the plasma storm."

"Excellent," Kyle murmured. "And what did you come up with?"

"Strangely enough, there were five disappearances of fourteen-year-olds in the days after the plasma storm. I eliminated three of them based on gender."

"Girls."

"Duh. Then I compared the other two to what we knew about the Mad Mask, deducing his height and weight based on his appearance. That gave me a match. Check it out."

Kyle removed Erasmus from his pouch and looked at the screen. On it was a lanky, laconic-looking teenager with watery blue eyes, a sharp little chin, and a chaotic thatch of dirty blond hair.

"This kid isn't disfigured. The Mad Mask is —"

"The picture predates his exposure to the radiation. It's before his disfigurement."

"Right. Who is he?"

"Meet Jack Stanley, fourteen years old. Parents Jerome and Johanna reported him missing a week after the plasma storm. Police found no signs of foul play, no note, nothing. He was just gone."

"Anything else?"

"There's a reward for him. Ten thousand bucks for information leading to his safe return home, quote-unquote. So maybe you can make a little dough while you're saving the town."

Kyle chuckled. "Not a bad idea. Okay, cool. Now we have some information. Good job, Erasmus. I'm impressed."

"Of course you are." Now that he'd imparted his information, Erasmus was back in full-on snark mode. "I've done *my* part, with consummate professionalism and impeccable timing, I might add. Now what are *you* going to do?"

Kyle only had to think about it for a moment. Not even a full moment, really — he had plenty of time left over in the moment to enjoy his plan.

"Me? I'm going to tear Ultitron to shreds. That'll definitely make the Mad Mask come crawling out of whatever hidey-hole he's sneaked away to. Plus, it has an added benefit: The whole town will see me defeat the robot that's threatening them. This time, it won't be like with the ASE — Mike won't get all the glory. I'll show them."

"Sounds good to me."

Kyle grinned. "Good. Let's go make some scrap metal."

Kyle dived through the clouds, his fists extended in front of him. He followed the sound of screams and emerged close to Ultitron. A huge ditch had been gouged out of the ground nearby, the spot where Ultitron had lain, buried and hidden, until activated by the Mad Mask. Kyle thought it looked like a grave for a ten-story-tall robot and promised himself that he would be burying Ultitron there soon enough.

The massive robot lurched toward the lighthouse, its huge feet kicking up tons of dirt and grass and the nice topiary Mairi's mom had paid way too much money to have planted around the grounds.

Kyle liked the topiary. Now he was even more ticked off.

Mighty Mike was a tiny blip circling Ultitron, lashing out with his black eye lasers, nudging the robot along. Every time Ultitron raised its arms to strike the lighthouse, Mike would zap it, causing the robot to swing around and thrash its enormous arms at him, forgetting about the lighthouse for the time being.

Safely stashed in a belt pouch again, Erasmus said, "Kyle, I'm picking up the police band. The Army and the National Guard are both on their way to Bouring. We're going to have a major shoot-out soon."

Great. That would make the exploding parking meters on Major Street look like a water balloon fight. The last thing Kyle needed was the military shooting up his hometown.

"Mike's clueless. I'm going to take out Ultitron right now."

"How do you plan on doing that? It has a force field almost as strong as the Mad Mask's."

Kyle rummaged in his belt pouch for some wires and batteries. He always kept basic electronic components in stock just in case. He also grabbed the Mad Mask's earplugs, which no longer worked but still had electronics he could scavenge.

"What are you doing?" Eramus asked.

"I helped build that thing. I especially helped with the motivational engine. I know how to disrupt its operations with a specific radio frequency." Kyle floated in the air, rapidly assembling pieces. "I'm going to build a transmitter."

"A remote kill-switch? Really?"

Kyle snorted. "I'm about to teach the Mad Mask a lesson in humility. Ah! Ha! Done!" He held up his newest creation — it was crude and slapped together quickly, resembling nothing so much as a ball of copper threads and small lights with a tiny, kinked wire sticking out of it like an antenna.

"Doesn't look like much, but it'll pack a wallop," Kyle said. "Ready to be a hero, Erasmus?"

"No one's going to know what *I* did," Erasmus sulked.

"Oh, don't be that way. When they throw me a parade for saving the town, I'll tell everyone you were instrumental in defeating the Mad Mask."

"Sure you will."

Kyle flew ahead. To his pleasure and amusement, Mighty Mike had just been struck by Ultitron's fist. The force of the punch, combined with the power of the force field, knocked Mike for a loop, sending him spinning off into the distance.

A crowd had gathered a safe distance from the lighthouse, commuters in stopped cars, Bouring residents rushing out of businesses and homes to watch the giant robot as it took a final menacing step. Nothing could stop it from swinging those powerful arms and destroying the lighthouse.

Nothing except Kyle.

He timed his approach perfectly, coming in from the south, where the big lights from the middle of town would backlight him very dramatically. No one could possibly miss him, and sure enough, people started pointing as he sped over town. They looked afraid, which made perfect sense because all they knew so far was what people like Mighty Mike told them. But once Kyle took care of Ultitron, they would stop being afraid. And when he showed up with the Mad Mask in custody and Mairi safe and sound, then — finally! — all this "Blue Freak" nonsense would stop and Kyle would be the Azure Avenger to one and all!

Total win-win scenario. Kyle couldn't lose.

Ultitron's head spun, blasting out with crisp red lasers. But Kyle knew they were coming — the motivational engine's programming was designed to try the lasers first. . . .

"Red wind is next," Kyle mumbled to himself.

Sure enough, a moment after he dodged the lasers, Ultitron opened its mouth and the fierce "red wind" blew forth, a potent combination of poisons and special nerve agents designed to paralyze and knock out anyone who inhaled it. But Kyle was ready for it, holding his breath and spinning rapidly in the air like a corkscrew, whipping up a savage wind of his own that dispersed the "red wind" harmlessly.

"Now!" he cried, kicking in the speed and pretending to punch Ultitron in the face as he triggered his killswitch. To the people of Bouring, it would look like he had knocked out Ultitron with a single punch, doing with one blow what Mighty Mike had been completely unable to do!

But nothing happened.

Kyle pulled up just before he slammed into Ultitron's force field. The air around the robot crackled with electricity and smelled faintly of ozone.

"What the heck . . . ?" Had he not hit the button? Sometimes it was tough to tell with his gloves on. He tried again.

Ultitron turned back to the lighthouse, still upright and functional.

"What's going on here?" Kyle wailed. He pressed the button again and again, floating in the air not far from Ultitron. It should have been working. "The motivational engine should be an inert piece of junk!"

"You were trying to break something," Erasmus said. "Given the usual efficacy of your gadgets, maybe you should have tried to improve it and then it would have broken."

"What are you talking about?" Kyle demanded, indignant.

"Pants Laser, anyone?"

"Shut up, Erasmus."

Mighty Mike blew past Kyle just then, his mouth set in a grim line. He blasted Ultitron with his eye lasers once more and blew at the robot with his Mighty Breath. Ultitron swatted Mike away.

"At this rate," Eramus went on, "Ultitron really does seem to be completely unstopp — Oh."

Mighty Mike tumbled past them, nearly colliding with Kyle. Kyle dashed aside, then soared in closer to Ultitron's head. Maybe he'd miscalculated the range on the kill-switch. Maybe he had to be right up against —

Ultitron's head swiveled toward Kyle again. Kyle braced himself for the lasers, but instead the robot's mouth opened. Kyle held his breath, ready for more "red wind."

And then Ultitron *spoke.* . . .

CHAPTER
FIFTEEN

Deep within his hidden lair, the Mad Mask stood before a gigantic HDTV screen connected to what looked like three computers and a game console that had been caught in a blender. The screen fed directly from Ultitron's eyes, showing what the robot saw, overlaid with a heads-up-display (HUD) that scrolled telemetry like distance to objective (in this case, the Bouring Lighthouse), fuel consumption (which was fine), and general maintenance parameters. Ultitron was — as expected — performing at, if not beyond, all projections. Truly, this was the single crowning achievement of robotics on the planet Earth.

As he watched, the costumed interloper designated "Mighty Mike" by the substandard popular media attempted to use his laser eyes on Ultitron's face. The Mad Mask touched a control and Ultitron blasted Mike away.

The Mad Mask chuckled under his mask, then remembered that he was in his own hidden lair and he could do whatever he wanted, so he laughed out loud, a hearty, sustained belly laugh that echoed up and down the concrete tunnels.

"You won't win," a small voice said.

The Mad Mask turned to see the girl — Mairi — behind him, still safely bound with heavy, flexible cables that had been left over from completing Ultitron. She could struggle, but she couldn't possibly escape.

"Oh? And your evidence for this unlikely scenario?" The Mad Mask decided to humor her.

"You're insane," she said, her green eyes flashing with resolve and anger. "Mighty Mike will stop you."

"Perhaps one in your particular position should find a kinder, gentler way of getting a point across," the Mad Mask said. He strode over to Mairi and took her chin in his hands, tilting her head so that she had no choice but to gaze into the eye slits cut into his mask. "One in your particular position, indeed, might consider inveigling oneself into the good graces of one's captor, rather than antagonizing said captor."

Mairi blinked. "I — I think I understand . . ." she said.

"That would be welcome and, in truth, quite surprising."

"You mean that I should —" and then she stopped long enough to hawk and spit a wad of saliva into the Mad Mask's face.

In disgust and rage, the Mad Mask reared back

and — before he could think about it — flung out one hand. A noxious gas jetted from a hidden nozzle behind his gauntlet. Mairi gasped, inhaling the gas. Her eyes rolled. She slumped in her restraints, her body slack and relaxed, unconscious.

With a corner of his cloak, the Mad Mask wiped her spittle from his mask. How dare she! How dare she *spit* in the face of the Mad Mask! He would — he would —

Just then, the screen caught the corner of his eye. He turned around to see none other than the Azure Avenger speeding toward Ultitron.

So. The security team at Lundergaard and Mighty Mike had not sufficed to eliminate the Azure Avenger.

The Mad Mask picked up a unit made from the fusion of a game console controller, a mouse, and a touch-screen cell phone. He slid his fingers across the controls, then held the device to his lips and said, "Attention, Azure Avenger . . ."

CHAPTER
SIXTEEN

". . . the Mad Mask has someone in his possession whom you care about very much!"

Kyle froze in midair at the sound of the voice. That was the Mad Mask's voice, broadcast through Ultitron!

"She is feisty, this one. Of that there can be no doubt."

Kyle smiled. Yeah, he couldn't picture Mairi going down without a fight. He figured she had already given the Mad Mask a tough time.

"In truth, she presents a dilemma," Ultitron/the Mad Mask went on. "What to do with her? Her strength could be . . . tempered, with proper psychological conditioning and overwhelming, muscular therapeutic intensity. . . ."

"You won't be able to brainwash her!" Kyle screamed. "She's too strong!"

A low chuckle came from Ultitron. The Mad Mask's chuckle had always been unnerving, but coming from the ten-story-tall robot, amplified by any number of speakers and woofers and tweeters, it was downright spine tingling.

"Everyone has a breaking point," the Mad Mask said, his voice so confident that Kyle could scarcely argue with him. "What makes you think she is any different?"

The Mad Mask had the brain-wave manipulator. Changing Mairi's personality would be almost trivially easy.

"I won't let you hurt her!" Kyle swore.

Again, that low chuckle that made the hair on the back of Kyle's neck stand up.

"You are willing to try, of course. You would, naturally, have to find her first. . . ."

Kyle couldn't hold back any longer. In a fury, in a red-blind rage, he plunged through the air at Ultitron, fists before him, ready to plow straight through the robot's head.

SPA-KOWWWW!

Instead, he screamed in agony as the force field crackled and snapped around him, hurling him higher into the air.

Ultitron laughed again. "Your function in the drama that is the Mad Mask's takeover and ruination of the world is over, Azure Avenger! You are and always have been surplus to requirements. Our partnership is at an end. All that remains now is to decide what to do with Mairi. Her beauty offends my advanced sensibilities. I should, by all rights, simply destroy her . . ."

Kyle screamed. He didn't scream "NO!" or "How

dare you!" or anything coherent at all. No, he simply screamed a pure, animalistic cry of anger, rage, defiance, and, ultimately, helplessness. He flew at Ultitron as fast as he could, not caring that he'd broken the sound barrier and caused a sonic boom that would rattle and shatter windows for miles around.

". . . or perhaps," Ultitron went on, "her spirit needs to be preserved, in which case, she should be hideously scarred so that she is worthy of standing as the Mad Mask's queen, ruling over the new, disfigured planet Earth!"

Kyle collided with Ultitron once again, knowing he would pay a penalty, but hoping that his unbound speed and strength would be enough to smash through that force field once and for all. Maybe it would kill him — probably it would kill him — but at least the momentum from his speed would carry his body through, tearing a hole through Ultitron's head. *Ha! Let's see him function after that!*

But as much as Kyle wanted to sacrifice himself for Mairi, he failed in this. The force field — that blasted, impossibly strong force field — still held. Pain seared him, like being electrocuted over and over while gigantic, molten-hot mallets pounded every inch of his body. He thought he heard the Mad Mask laugh as he bounced off the force field, his limbs spasming and jerking uncontrollably.

The last thing he saw before he blacked out was a green-and-gold blur on the horizon.

Thank God, he thought. *Mighty Mike*.

And then the shock of that thought — and the ocean of pain — knocked him out.

Kyle awakened in a crater of crumbled asphalt to one side of Kimota Road, miles and miles from Ultitron. A cautious crowd of onlookers gathered around him. As he groaned and propped himself up on his elbows, everyone took a step back at once, as if they were all attached to the same marionette strings and the puppeteer had just yanked.

"It's really *him*," someone said. "The Blue Freak."

An undercurrent of agreement, awe, and worry rippled through the crowd. Kyle was in too much pain to correct them.

"Are you all right?" Erasmus crackled in his ear. One of the plugs had been damaged — he was only receiving static in his left ear. It was like listening to Erasmus with the shower running in the background.

"I'm all right." He managed to get into a sitting position and that was about it for now. Every muscle in his body hurt. Every *bone* in his body hurt. Kyle was pretty sure even his glands and skin hurt.

"Help him up!" someone said. "He was fighting that thing!"

"Are you nuts? The FBI and Homeland Security are after him. He probably built that thing!" someone else replied.

As the crowd argued among itself — proving to Kyle once again that great things never happen when you get more than a couple of people together; greatness happens alone — Kyle strained and grunted until he was standing. His costume was still intact, but it had fresh tears and scorch marks all along it. His own breath tasted and smelled sour in the confines of his mask, so he knew his face was still concealed. Thank God for small favors.

"Look!" someone shouted, and Kyle held up a hand to forestall any applause at his monumental task of standing up on his own, only to realize that the "Look!" didn't refer to him. He followed a dozen pointing fingers to the sky, not that it was necessary — the sound of rotor blades and engines was clue enough.

The Army had arrived. Finally.

Apache attack helicopters dropped into formation over Bouring, flanked by what looked like a small flotilla of Predator drones, unmanned, remote-controlled death machines. Kyle laughed at the irony. The military was sending in a fleet of robots to fight a robot. He didn't give them very good odds.

The crowd hustled closer to the action, Kyle forgotten. He couldn't believe these idiots. Clearly terrified and undoubtedly out of their league, they were still getting closer to the danger, not farther away. And why? To get a better look. To shoot video with their cell phones. Nincompoops. At the first explosion, they would run pell-mell for cover, probably trampling each other.

Kyle called out for them to head in the other direction instead, to safety, but his voice was weak and he had no strength to yell. Fine. Let them suffer their fate. It was the cruelest iteration of the Prankster Manifesto: These people who took themselves so seriously would pay the ultimate . . .

A booming noise from overhead shattered the darkening sky, sending fireworks and flares in every direction. Ultitron had just zapped an Apache and the helicopter had spun out of control, careening smack into the giant robot, where it exploded into a million flaming pieces. Kyle's eyes widened, his throat tight with sudden grief until he saw Mighty Mike swooping away from the wreckage, the two Army pilots tucked safely under his arms. It was comical — a kid-size body hauling two full-grown adults — but right now Kyle could find nothing funny about it.

The street rumbled. Tanks would be on the way. Maybe the combined might of Mighty Mike and the military could stop Ultitron, but Kyle doubted it. Only one thing could do that, he knew:

The Mad Mask.

But how could he get to him? The Mad Mask had to be operating from somewhere nearby, Kyle knew. Whether he was using Wi-Fi or a special microwave link to Ultitron, it would only work over short distances — five or six miles at the most. Still, five or six miles in each direction from Ultitron . . . That made for a circle with a diameter of up to twelve miles and a total area of, uh, πr^2, which worked out to over 113 square miles of —

Gah! He grabbed his head as if that would shut off the endlessly calculating part of his brain. He needed all of his brainpower, all of his focus on finding the Mad Mask somewhere in that 113-square-mile range of places. Even a tiny town like Bouring had thousands of buildings to hide in. . . .

Off in the distance, the crowd that had been around him was now way too close to the danger zone. Against his better judgment, Kyle figured he should save them from themselves. He looked around for something to throw at them, to make them scatter, and found only a manhole cover, knocked partly loose from the road by the force of his crash landing. That would do.

Kyle lifted the one-hundred-pound steel disc as if it weighed nothing. "Hey!" he shouted, finding his voice again. "Watch this!"

The crowd, hearing him now, turned just in time to watch him whip the cover toward them like a Frisbee. Of course, he was very careful because he wanted to scare them, not hurt them. He made sure to give it the right amount of loft and twist so that it would spin up into the air overhead and land harmlessly on the other side of the street.

But it worked — they didn't realize they weren't in any danger, and the crowd split up and ran for cover.

Good. He put his fists on his hips and turned in a slow circle. *If I were the Mad Mask, which building would I —*

No. Wait a second. Kyle's math was wrong. The blow from Ultitron and the rough landing must have rattled his brains more than he thought.

The formula πr^2 was for the *area* of a *circle*, a two-dimensional space. But this was the real world. It wasn't flat — it was *three*-dimensional. (Actually, it was four-dimensional and maybe as much as thirteen-dimensional, but Kyle didn't have time for that right now.) The Mad Mask's microwave link could go five to six miles in *any* direction. That meant up or down, too, he told Erasmus.

The AI's voice crackled and hissed: "He could **ftz** anywhere **ftzzzzz** sphere with a **crrtzl** —"

"With a volume of $4/3(\pi r^3)$ which works out to over nine hundred cubic miles, but . . ." The enormity of scouring that much territory before Ultitron could be contained . . . Even at Kyle's speed, it seemed impossible. He would have to look high and low. . . .

"Up *kzzzrkll* down," Erasmus suggested.

Yes, up and . . .

And down . . .

Kyle looked down at his feet. At the crater he'd made in the road when he'd landed.

At the open sewer hole.

Down.

An open sewer hole . . .

He thought of the gigantic trench where Ultitron had awaited activation, concealed *underground.* . . . The robot had been underground all along. . . .

"Of course," Kyle whispered. "He hates beauty . . . So why wouldn't he . . ."

"*kzrtl* in filth," Erasmus said. Kyle got tired of the static and popped out the earbud that was damaged. Now he couldn't hear Erasmus in stereo anymore, but at least he was clear.

It made perfect sense that the Mad Mask would have his lair underground, in the sewers. Decision time: Should he head back out and try to help Mike destroy Ultitron or should he go after Mairi?

There was no other option. Sure, he could join Mighty Mike and the Army and maybe together they could all beat Ultitron, but he doubted it. Besides, he wasn't about to make the same mistake he'd made with the ASE. That time, he let Mairi stay in danger while he ran off to save the planet. End result? Mighty Mike became more popular than ever and Kyle ended up a fugitive from the law. This time, he would find Mairi and rescue her . . . and drag the secret to deactivating Ultitron out of the Mad Mask. There was no downside.

"Here we go, Erasmus," Kyle said, and hopped into the sewer before he could think of a reason not to.

CHAPTER
SEVENTEEN

Kyle had a pretty good imagination, but the sewer was even grosser than he had imagined. The walls crawled with muck; the ceiling and the pipes sweated drops of foul liquid. It smelled like a bathroom had thrown up.

The concrete conduit ran north to south, and each direction was nothing but filthy water with stuff floating in it. Kyle didn't want to spend too much time thinking about what the stuff was.

"Have you got a schematic of the town sewer system?" he asked Erasmus.

"I'm not sure," Erasmus admitted, his voice small and tinny through the lone earbud. "I had to off-load a lot of data to make room for Ultitron's schematics. Let me look."

"Hurry. I don't want to waste time going the wrong way. And pump your volume while you're at it. I'm having trouble hearing you."

Kyle took a step forward and immediately regretted it as his foot sank up to the ankle in something thick and sucking that was much more than just liquid. He pulled back and hovered a few inches over the river of sheer gross that flowed under him. The sewer was only six feet in diameter, so he didn't have a lot of room, but he would rather bang his head than step in that . . . stuff again.

"Anything?" he asked Erasmus, peering ahead into the darkness. The open manhole was right above him and even though it was rapidly darkening outside, it was still brighter in this little spot than anywhere else, where total black enveloped the sewer. Kyle shifted the lenses in his mask to ultraviolet and groaned — now he could see (in the bright green tones of night vision) the grotesque oozing stream below his feet as it slowly flowed south, as well as rusting, sewage-sweating pipes that ran along the sides of the conduit.

He could also see a family of rats the size of small dogs clustered a few yards to the south, clinging to the pipes and staring at him. Just terrific.

"Erasmus . . ." he sing-songed.

"I have some of the blueprints," Erasmus chimed in, his voice louder but unbalanced, causing Kyle to tilt his head to the right, "although not all of them. Bad news is that there are a number of large intersection chambers where the Mad Mask could set up a command center of some sort. We'll have to check them one at a time."

Just then, the ground shook and the fetid air vibrated. Jets thundered overhead and tanks came onto the streets of Bouring. Kyle heard the *kuh-BOOM-BOOM!* of the big repeating cannons on the tanks.

"We don't have much time. Ultitron's gonna wipe out the Army if the Army doesn't wipe out the town first. Collateral damage. Scan the blueprints for the chambers that are easiest to access from the surface."

"Okay, but it doesn't matter," Erasmus protested. "The Mad Mask could just teleport into any of them, so the easiest ones are —"

"But he can't teleport something as big as Ultitron, I don't think. So he would have to be near . . . by . . ." He drifted off.

"But Kyle, you can't be sure that —"

"Hush!" Kyle told Erasmus. Something . . . something was right on the tip of his tongue.

"What do you mean, hush?" Erasmus said indignantly. "I will not —"

Kyle clawed up his mask on his right side and pulled out the earbud for some silence.

Something Erasmus had said . . . about teleporting . . .

Kyle closed his eyes. Teleporting. The Mad Mask could teleport anywhere, couldn't he? So he could teleport to his lair no matter where . . .

But wait.

If the Mad Mask could teleport . . .

(And he could — hadn't Kyle witnessed it himself near the lighthouse that day?)

195

If he could teleport, then why . . .

If he could teleport.

If.

He couldn't, Kyle realized. The Mad Mask couldn't actually teleport.

He remembered the first time he'd seen the Mad Mask, how the Mad Mask had watched Kyle fly away. At first Kyle thought he was ashamed that he couldn't fly, too. Then, later, he thought the Mad Mask just didn't want Kyle to see him teleport yet. But now . . .

Kyle popped the earbud back in and pulled down his mask.

"He didn't want me to see him *walk* away," Kyle said, interrupting Erasmus, who was still rattling off a litany of offenses Kyle had perpetrated against him.

". . . constantly telling me to shut up and to — Wait, what did you say?"

"And if he could teleport," Kyle went on, "he would have done it today. He would have gone straight from Lundergaard to my house. But he stole that car and drove. Which means he can't teleport."

"You *saw* —"

"I saw a flash of bright light and then the Mad Mask appeared. He must have been nearby, waiting. The light distracted me and then he just walked over while I was blinded."

"Walked over from where?"

Kyle grinned even though Erasmus couldn't see it. "From the sewer outlet near the lighthouse."

Erasmus didn't need to breathe, but just for the sake of verisimilitude, he made a sound like someone inhaling sharply. "Oh. Oh! Oh! Kyle, there's a *huge* sewer conduit right near the lighthouse. . . ."

"And that's where Ultitron first showed up . . ."

"*And* where Ultitron lay before being activated . . ."

"Which means the Mad Mask had to be in the same place in order to work on Ultitron . . ."

"That's where he is!" Erasmus cried, as proud-sounding as if he'd come up with it all on his own.

"South!" Kyle shouted, and flew. The rats scattered, some of them scampering off along the pipes, some of them dropping to splash to safety through the raw sewage. Kyle's night-vision lenses kept him from being totally in the dark, but the strange green shadows and the twists and bends of the tunnels made it slow going. Pipes and wheels jutted out of the walls and ceiling at seemingly random points, forcing Kyle to duck and dodge as he flew. Soon, he was actually panting — not from exertion, but just from having to breathe through his mouth. The stench was terrible.

"I am so glad I don't have a nose," Erasmus said.

"I would totally trade places with you right now," Kyle admitted, and kept flying through the tunnels, doing his best to avoid the slime and general grossness. But he couldn't help it entirely — *stuff* dripped from the ceiling and occasionally he would brush against a grimy pipe or stretch of conduit. He was going to have to invent a whole new kind of washing machine to clean his costume after this disaster. It would probably involve a high-powered laser. Just about everything could be improved by adding a high-powered laser.

He felt like he'd been flying for hours, even though Erasmus assured him it had only been minutes. The tunnels branched off and twisted and turned unexpectedly. Erasmus's GPS couldn't work underground, so Kyle had to rely on his own sense of direction and on Erasmus's partial blueprints of the sewer system, hoping that he was headed the right way.

And just then, something emerged up ahead, and he knew he was where he needed to be.

It was the Mad Mask!

Kyle pulled up, hovering in the dank, fetid depths of the sewer, then flattened himself against the wall, no matter how disgusting it was. (He actually *squished* when he pressed into it and tried not to think about that.)

"What are you doing?" Erasmus whispered.

"I don't think he saw me. His eyes aren't green. His night vision is off."

It was strange to see the Mad Mask just . . . standing

there, in the midst of all that muck and sewage. Some filthy water dripped on him from above, but the Mad Mask just stood there.

"Something's wrong," Kyle said. "The Mad Mask would never just stand there and let grungy water get all over his cloak. . . ."

The Mad Mask moved; he turned to the left, walked a few feet in that direction, and stopped. Then he turned to the left again, walked, stopped. He did this two more times, making a perfect square that brought him right back to where he'd started.

As Kyle watched, he did it again. Every thirty-two seconds, the cycle started again.

It's a robot, Kyle realized. It wasn't really the Mad Mask, just . . . an android designed to look like him. A . . . a MadDroid.

It's standing guard. I must be in the right place.

Before he could think about it any more, Kyle pushed off from the wall and launched himself through the air at the MadDroid. He got within a foot before the thing realized he was there, looking up just as Kyle collided with it, driving them both back along the tunnel and into the filthy river of muck.

"Unhand the Mad Mask!" the MadDroid cried out in a reasonable facsimile of the real deal's voice. "The Mad Mask is not to be manhandled by lesser mortals such as you!"

"Wow, he even programmed it to be as obnoxious as he is!" Erasmus marveled.

"Go figure," Kyle grunted as he wrestled with the MadDroid in the filth. The robot was incredibly strong. Fortunately, it didn't seem to have a force field, so he was able to pummel it as much as he wanted.

"What kind of an egomaniac builds a robot that talks just like him?" Erasmus asked.

"Can we talk about this later?" Kyle asked, struggling to keep the MadDroid from choking him. He grabbed its wrists and pushed with his knees, trying to shove it away from him. The stupid thing wouldn't let go.

"Such egomania reveals interesting things about the Mad Mask's pathology," Erasmus went on.

"Fighting for my life here!" Kyle kicked at the MadDroid, finally loosening its grip. He lashed out with his other foot and knocked the thing back several feet, then regained his footing and lunged at it. The MadDroid tried to fend him off, but Kyle managed to duck under its arms, tackling it in the gut and driving it back against the tunnel wall, where it split in two. The legs dropped into the muck and the top half collapsed onto Kyle's back, then slipped off and joined the legs.

Kyle was so relieved that he barely noticed the filth and sewage streaming off his costume. He had expected the robot to be a much, much more difficult opponent. What the heck had the Mad Mask built this thing out of, anyway?

Kyle crouched down and rummaged in the sewage until he found the MadDroid's arm. He knew he should be rushing to the Mad Mask's lair, but he couldn't help it — his curiosity just wouldn't let it go.

He hauled the torso out of the slime — the shoulder joint snapped and the torso splashed back down, leaving Kyle holding only the arm. What kind of cheap stuff was the Mad Mask using to build —?

He examined the arm. It was . . .

That was impossible.

It looked like it was just a store mannequin's arm! With some padding added, yeah, but still just a run-of-the-mill mannequin.

Kyle ripped off the mask. Unlike the Mad Mask's, this one was made out of cheap plastic. Underneath, the mannequin's face had been hollowed out. A rats' nest of wires and cables sat balled-up in the cavity. When he pawed at the mess, it popped out. The wires weren't attached to anything. They were just stuffed in there. What was the point? How the heck did something like this even *work* —

"Oh," Kyle said out loud. "Oh."

"What?" Erasmus asked. "Shouldn't we get moving?"

"I just figured it out," Kyle said in a soft voice. "Everything makes sense now. I figured out the Mad Mask's secret."

"I didn't know he had a secret."

"Everyone has a secret." Kyle dropped the arm. "It's time to go."

CHAPTER
EIGHTEEN

Kyle tore through the tunnel as fast as he dared, dodging low-hanging pipes and scaring what looked like an entire army of rats. Who knew Bouring had so many rats? (Kyle filed that fact away — he would need to create some kind of rat-killing ray someday. Just because.)

Now that he knew the truth about the Mad Mask, nothing was going to keep him from doing what Mighty Mike couldn't: stopping Ultitron and rescuing Mairi and putting an end to the Mad Mask's scheme once and for all.

A platoon of MadDroids waited just ahead. Past them, Kyle could see a large archway filled with light. The archway was slightly elevated from the rest of the sewer, so it would be clean and dry. The Mad Mask would be there, Kyle knew.

He flailed through the MadDroids. They grabbed and scraped and clawed at him, but he kicked and thrashed and threw punches. Now that he knew they were nothing more than glorified dummies, he wasn't afraid of them. He fought his way through them until he felt solid concrete under his feet, then forged ahead, a dozen MadDroids clinging to him and trying to bear him down.

Finally, he stepped into the light.

The chamber was large, with a concrete floor and a massive flagged stone dome. Tunnels ran in and out from all directions. In the center of the room was a gigantic HDTV screen, on which Kyle could see Ultitron fighting off the military and Mighty Mike. Standing in front of the screen was, of course, the Mad Mask — the real deal this time.

And off in a corner was . . .

"Mairi!" Kyle screamed. He couldn't help it. She was slumped against the wall, her eyes closed, her breathing shallow.

Kyle moved toward her, but the MadDroids tangled him up in their grasp and held him back.

The Mad Mask turned away from his screen, his stance erect, his hands clasped behind his back as usual. "Ah. Azure Avenger. Your tenacity and will are more impressive than the Mad Mask had imagined. Ultimately, however, they are and always have been for naught! You have arrived only in time to witness the victory of Ultitron and the first of many triumphs of the Mad Mask!"

"If you've hurt Mairi . . ." Kyle strained against the MadDroids, but there were too many of them. And besides, he knew why they were so tough to beat right at this moment, compared to the one in the tunnel.

"Hurt her? She rests. I merely tired of her prattle. She is to be my queen. To be sure, a most appropriate and fitting disfigurement will be chosen for her. Once her beauty has been eradicated, she will be a fit queen for the Mad Mask." He chuckled and picked something up from a table. "And once she's been exposed to this, of course, her attitude will change quite dramatically. . . ."

The brain-wave manipulator!

"And now here you are, Azure Avenger, come to save the day, you most likely imagine." The Mad Mask shook his head and tsked. "Do your worst! The triumph of the Mad Mask is preordained!"

"Oh, shut up," Kyle said. "I've got you figured out."

"You? Have 'figured out' the Mad Mask? Ha! Your intellect is mighty, this is true, but it is a snow-flake compared to the blizzard of the Mad Mask's brainpo —"

"Shut up!" Kyle yelled. "You're not a genius! You never have been. You're an idiot!"

For a moment, there was no sound, no speaking, nothing. The Mad Mask put the brain-wave manipulator back on the table.

"Take. That. Back," he said icily.

"No. I won't. It's the truth. You're a moron." Kyle flexed his muscles. The MadDroids gave . . . just a little.

"And in a few seconds, I'm going to break free from your pets here and rip your mask off."

If the Mad Mask was scared, he didn't show it, though he did pause for a moment before responding. "My force field will —"

"Your force field? What force field? There is no force field! None that you built, at least. You couldn't build a LEGO set if your life depended on it."

"Brave words for someone currently held back by the Mad Mask's genius in the science of robotics!"

"These aren't robots, you moron! They're just store mannequins that you messed with. You added some wiring and some electronics to make them look like robots, but they're not. They're nothing, Jack!"

"What did you call me?"

"I called you Jack. Jack Stanley. That's your name."

The Mad Mask took a step backward, as if a large, invisible hand had just shoved him. "Stop . . . Don't use that name."

"Why not, Jack? It's your name, after all."

Kyle noticed that the MadDroids' grip on him had slackened. They were shutting down, for lack of a better word.

"Your gadgets don't really work," Kyle said, pushing forward. It was like walking against a blizzard . . . if the blizzard actually had hands that could grab and pull at you. "They only work because you *think* they work. That's how these mannequins walk around. That's why your special earplugs stopped working when you drove out of range at Lundergaard. Heck, even the bug you planted on me was probably just something you bought at a store — you were only able to track me because your receiver was near you."

"Stop it!" the Mad Mask screamed. He held out a threatening hand. "MadDroids! Crush him! Destroy him!"

Kyle shrugged off the MadDroids like lint. "That's why I couldn't make sense of your schematics — they were just garbage. The motivational engine didn't work when I put it together. It didn't work until *you* came over to my house! You just needed me as a distraction, a way to keep Mighty Mike off your back when you activated Ultitron."

"The radiation . . ." Erasmus realized. "It didn't give him a heightened intellect at all. It gave him the psychic power to control electronics." Erasmus paused. "And drove him a little nutty, too, I guess."

The Mad Mask took another step back. One of the MadDroids made a feeble attempt to grab Kyle by the ankle, but Kyle easily kicked it away, severing the arm in the process. Now that he'd shaken the Mad Mask's faith in his own skills, his gadgets were starting to fail.

"Impossible . . ." the Mad Mask said. If Kyle could have seen his eyes behind that mask, he imagined they'd be wide with terror.

The Mad Mask spun around to look at his screen. "It's impossible!" he screamed. "Impossible! I am the Mad Mask! I am —"

"You are Jack Stanley!" Kyle shouted.

The Mad Mask flinched as if he'd been bashed in the back of the head with a shovel. At the same moment, on the screen, Ultitron wavered and staggered, suddenly no longer potent. Two Army Sidewinder missiles fired from Apache helicopters exploded along its chest. An instant later, Mighty Mike rocketed past . . .

And ripped off the thing's arms.

Kyle couldn't help it — he wanted to cheer for Mighty Mike.

"No!" screamed the Mad Mask. "It cannot be! It *will not* be!" He spun back around to Kyle. "I am the Mad Mask! I am the Mad Mask!"

The horde of MadDroids suddenly came to life, pummeling Kyle. He swiped at them viciously with fists and feet, not holding back. They were powerful, but not nearly as powerful as before — the Mad Mask's control was slipping. On the viewscreen, Kyle could see Ultitron moving again, staggering away from the lighthouse but right toward a big shopping center. Its force field was back up, and Mike couldn't get near it again.

"Jack Stanley!" he shouted again. "You're just Jack Stanley!" A MadDroid sank its hand into Kyle's mask and tore away most of the face covering, but he kept shouting the Mad Mask's real name.

The Mad Mask looked from Kyle to the viewscreen and back again. Then, in a panic, he bolted for one of the tunnels.

"No way!" Kyle said. "You're not getting away that easily!" He shook off the remaining MadDroids, even as one of them stripped away the rest of his mask. He dived for the Mad Mask, missed, ended up near the table with . . . with . . .

The brain-wave manipulator.

Kyle grabbed the manipulator. "Hey, Jack!" he shouted.

The Mad Mask spun around. Kyle grinned; he could imagine the look of sudden horror under that ebony mask.

"No!" the Mad Mask yelled, but Kyle had already triggered the device.

"You're Jack Stanley. You're not a robotics genius. You don't even remember building Ultitron. Or my real name. Forget it all. Forget your powers. Forget —"

The Mad Mask cried out and collapsed, pointing behind Kyle. Kyle turned to see Ultitron, frozen on the screen, balanced precariously on one foot, the other one raised, ready to stomp on the shopping center.

Truthfully, Bouring would probably be better off without another shopping center, but Kyle was still psyched that he'd managed to save the day.

He dropped the brain-wave manipulator on the table and advanced on the Mad Mask, who cowered against the wall. "No, please . . ."

"All of your so-called 'technology' is failing," Kyle said. He reached down and grabbed the Mad Mask by the front of his shirt, dragging him up to his feet. "Even your force field. It's all failing you. Now we're going to see what you're hiding under that mask!"

"No!" the Mad Mask whimpered. "Please!"

"Oh, be quiet. You lost. Deal with it."

The Mad Mask wriggled and struggled, helpless in Kyle's grasp. "I beg you! Please! You cannot reveal this heinous visage to the world!"

But with his free hand, Kyle grabbed the chin of the mask and pulled it off . . .

. . . and . . .

"You're kidding me!" Kyle yelled, shoving the Mad Mask away from him. "It's just a pimple!"

The Mad Mask curled into a ball on the floor and covered his face.

"Don't look at it!" he cried. "It's hideous! I'm hideous!"

Kyle couldn't believe it. "Oh, for God's sake . . ."

"It's all white and crusty on top!" the Mad Mask went on. "And . . . and . . . I think there's a hair growing out of it!"

"You're kidding," Kyle said again.

"Wait," the Mad Mask said, sniffling. "We can work together. . . . Just give me back my mask and we can —"

"Are you insane? No, wait, don't bother — I already know the answer to that question."

Kyle tossed the mask aside and turned to the viewscreen.

Just then, a new voice: "Kyle?"

Mairi was awake!

CHAPTER
NINETEEN

"I . . . I can explain everything . . ." Kyle said, hesitating at first.

But one look at the shock and hurt and betrayal in Mairi's eyes forced him to question his confidence. There was no way he could explain this that would make it all better. The expression on Mairi's face communicated more than just surprise or anger or any one emotion. Any single emotion he could have handled, but the combination of them all was too much.

He was busted, plain and simple. His greatest secret was out, and to the one person in the world who had always believed in him. For the first time in a long time, Kyle felt ashamed of himself.

He was going to keep talking — he didn't know what he was going to say, but somehow it had just become enormously important that he keep talking, no matter what. Maybe if he kept blathering on, Mairi would never get the chance to yell at him or tell him how angry and disappointed she was. But before he could speak, a scurrying sound caught his attention.

Kyle turned just in time to see the Mad Mask rabbiting, that long cloak vanishing into one of the multitude of tunnels that intersected the lair. Kyle moved to follow but stopped when he caught sight of the big viewscreen: On it, Ultitron, still frozen in mid-stomp, teetered, totally unbalanced (probably because Mighty Mike ripped off its arms, the chump — when would Mike use his brain and realize that you can't just rip limbs off of giant robots without thinking through the consequences? Like always, Mike only did half the job).

A ten-story-tall creature made of metal and who-knows-what kind of dangerous materials was about to collapse on the town!

Kyle spun back to Mairi. "Stay here," he told her. As if she had a choice — where would she go? "You'll be safe for now. I'll be back. I promise."

The last thing he saw before darting into a tunnel was the look on Mairi's face: the rage. The disbelief.

The total and complete lack of trust in Kyle.

He sped through the tunnels as quickly as he could, once again ducking and dodging pipes. There was probably a shortcut to the surface, but Kyle had decided to simply reverse the path he'd taken to the lair because he knew the route already. Rats ran before him like a vanguard, and Kyle allowed himself for a moment to imagine how cool it would be to create a gadget that would make rats do his bidding. . . .

"Nearing the opening," Erasmus reported. "Time to mask up."

"Right."

Kyle's own mask had been shredded by the MadDroids, but he'd snatched up the Mad Mask's ebony-and-ivory mask right before leaving the lair. Jack Stanley, in his panic, had fled without it, leaving it on the floor where Kyle had dropped it.

Now Kyle slipped the Mad Mask's face over his own, then popped up from the street into the chaos of Bouring.

It was worse than he'd imagined, worse than he'd seen on the viewscreen. The town was a disaster movie happening in real life, people running every which way as Army tanks and platoons of soldiers marched through town, helicopters and Predators buzzing overhead. And there, just off in the distance, the massive form of Ultitron, the most useless robot in history, tipping precariously. Any second now it would collapse. Kyle quickly calculated azimuths and trajectories and triangulations. It was going to crush not just buildings but also people! He had to move quickly —

But even as he started toward Ultitron, the robot creaked to a halt in midair, poised shakily on the tips of its toes but not falling anymore.

Mighty Mike.

When Kyle focused, he could see the tiny figure of Mighty Mike against the enormous bulk of Ultitron. The entire town went silent. Even the Army guys shut up. It was, Kyle had to admit, pretty amazing to see — Mighty Mike single-handedly (well, with both hands, but by himself) bracing the entire weight of Ultitron.

And then — after that silent moment — Mike heaved. Even from here, Kyle imagined he could hear Mike grunt, see the strain and the bulge of his muscles as he did the impossible and lifted Ultitron entirely off the ground.

A cheer went up from the crowd. Kyle snorted. They were applauding too soon. If Mike dropped Ultitron now, the devastation would still be —

After a hovering moment, Mike put on a burst of strength and speed, hauling Ultitron up and away from Bouring. The applause intensified. Kyle watched him go. Mike would probably go dump Ultitron near the old coal mine, where it could later be dismantled without causing harm to anyone. He sighed. His help wasn't needed after all.

"Blue Freak!" someone shouted, and Kyle looked around just as the same voice shouted, "All units! Open fire!"

The next thing Kyle knew, he was in a cloud of ammunition. Bullets. Rocket-propelled grenades. The real stuff. Nothing fake here. This was the Army.

The United States Army had just opened fire on Kyle. For real.

Explosions and impacts buffeted him in the air, tossing him back and forth, up and down. He raised an arm to shield his face, even though he was wearing the ebony mask.

"Stop it!" he yelled. "I'm here to help!" But no one could hear him over the unending roar of munitions.

"Kyle, even your body can only handle so much punishment. . . ."

Erasmus was right. Kyle knew he had no choice but to retreat. He could just fly away, but that would leave Mairi abandoned in the sewers. Plus, those helicopters and drones would just follow him wherever he went.

So it was back into the sewers. He dropped down into the filth and the stink.

Kyle drifted along the smelly air currents in the sewer, back toward what had been the Mad Mask's lair. The rats had apparently gotten used to him invading their territory — they barely even looked at him as he glided by.

The Army was taking its sweet time coming down after him. That made sense. They didn't want to go charging blind into an unfamiliar situation, especially when a "bad guy" was ready and waiting for them.

"What are you going to do about Mairi?" Erasmus asked.

"I have no idea," Kyle admitted. They were the four hardest words he'd ever assembled into a sentence.

"What are you going to say to her?"

"I'll explain things to her. It'll take awhile. But she'll understand." That was the extent of his plan right now: Leave a trail to the lair that even the Army could follow. Explain things to Mairi. Escape through another tunnel. Let the Army rescue Mairi so that they felt like they accomplished something other than dropping a metric ton of live ordnance on Bouring. It wasn't the greatest plan in the world, but it ended with Kyle safe and Mairi rescued, so that was all that mattered.

"You know, when they get to her, they're going to ask her questions. About you."

"I know. She won't give me up," Kyle said confidently. "Not Mairi. She's my friend —"

"Exactly. Are you going to put her through that? Make her lie to everyone about you? Are you going to make her live with the knowledge that her best friend is a wanted criminal, the most dangerous person on the planet?"

Grr. "No. No, I guess not."

"You know what you have to do," Erasmus said ominously.

Kyle clenched his fists. Yeah. Yeah, he knew what he had to do.

Kyle drifted into the Mad Mask's abandoned control center. In one hand, he held the ebony mask; he held the other out in what he hoped was a calming gesture. Mairi had gotten up from her position on the ground and was now over by the viewscreen, which had gone dead when the Mad Mask fled. Mairi was fiddling with the controls, trying to coax the system back to life. Kyle didn't have the heart to tell her that it had never really worked — the whole system had been powered by the Mad Mask's belief in it. Once he stopped thinking about it, once he was out of range, it all became junk.

"Mairi," he said as calmly as he could.

She spun around, and the terror in her eyes hurt Kyle a thousand times more than all the rockets the Army had fired at him.

"Stay away from me!" She backed up against the console.

"Mairi, I'm not going to —"

"Stay away!" she screamed. "Stay away! You lied to me! You left me to die!"

She was talking about the ASE, he knew. She didn't know — no one knew — that Kyle had left Mighty Mike to rescue her from the ASE because there was something more important to do: absorbing the radiation that was *causing* the ASE before it spread to the entire town and the whole world.

"I knew Mike would save you. I had to go and —"

"I don't want to hear it, Kyle." She edged to the left, moving toward one of the tunnels. Kyle moved that way, too. He couldn't let her get into the tunnels. She could easily get lost in there and never make her way out. "You lied to me. You tried to kill Mike on Mighty Mike Day. You trashed the town. You left me to die with the dirt monster. And then you teamed up with this lunatic who kidnapped me!"

"Wow," Erasmus said, "when you put it that way, you sound pretty bad!"

"Shut up!" Kyle said. As usual, when there was no immediate danger, Erasmus wasn't being very helpful.

"Don't tell me to shut up!" Mairi yelled. "I thought you were my friend!"

"I am your friend —"

"Friends don't try to kill each other!"

Kyle moved to his left a bit. He could see his goal now. He was very close, but he didn't want to startle Mairi and make her do something stupid.

"I never tried to kill you, Mairi. I'm trying to help you."

"You expect me to believe you? Do you really expect me to ever believe *anything* you ever say again?"

Kyle made his move, snatching the brain-wave manipulator from the table where he'd left it. Before Mairi could move — or his own conscience could interrupt — Kyle aimed it at Mairi and triggered the device. "Don't move," he told her, and Mairi froze in place, her face still twisted into anger and hate.

"You won't remember that Kyle Camden is the Blue Freak," he told her.

"Who?" she said, her eyes suddenly heavy and dreamy.

"Kyle," Erasmus interrupted, "I'm picking up radio chatter nearby. The Army is closing in."

Kyle stared at Mairi. Was he really doing this? Was he really altering Mairi's brain? It had been one thing to make his parents think a little differently — they were parents. But this was Mairi. She had trusted him, once. And now he was . . .

"Kyle!" Erasmus yelled in the one remaining earbud, cranking up the volume.

"You will forget you saw my face," Kyle told Mairi.

"Whose face?" she asked, sounding sleepy.

There was so much more he wanted to do. So much more he could do. But he didn't have the time.

"Go to sleep," he told her, and Mairi yawned, then stretched out on the floor and drifted off into a peaceful sleep. Kyle stood over her, watching.

Then — before he could change his mind — he destroyed the brain-wave manipulator, crushing it into a ball of twisted metal with his bare hands.

"What did you do that for?" Erasmus yelped. "I just fixed it!"

"I never want to be able to make this choice again," Kyle said soberly.

From down one of the tunnels, he could hear them now, the soldiers, splashing through the muck.

Kyle picked a different tunnel and flew into it. He knew that he could take the sewers to a spot outside of town and escape that way. His plans had failed, but once again he would escape to fight another day.

As he'd thought when this all began, his plans might not always work, but at least his escapes were always . . .

He flew through the dank, reeking darkness. Yeah. Slogging through the sewer was a really spectacular escape.

from the top secret journal of
Kyle Camden (deciphered):

A week later, and the town of Bouring is beginning to recover from the attack of Ultitron.

And, might I add, the attack of the Army. Those guys caused almost as much damage as Ultitron did.

Mighty Mike, of course, was instrumental in the repair work. Why bring in a bunch of cranes to lift building materials when Mike can do it? Why hoist guys up to the top of a roof to nail down slate when Mike can float up there and drive nails with his bare hands? And if he sometimes uses too much strength and breaks the slate or puts his fist through a new wall? Well, who cares, everyone says — he's a good kid! He means well.

Feh.

He even helped raise money for the reconstruction by auctioning off superpowered feats. One rich computer mogul from California paid fifty thousand dollars on eBay to have Mighty Mike fly him up into the stratosphere in a space suit.

(I've been to the stratosphere. It's no big deal.)

He also helped soothe everyone's frazzled nerves by performing superfeats, including flying some kids around town, just to give them a thrill.

Of course, he took Mairi on an extra-long flight,

much to the delight of the crowd. "Mairi has suffered more than anyone else in this," he told the Bouring Record. "She was napped by the evil villains who created the robot and left in the sewers by herself."

No one bothered to correct his "napped" gaffe. At this point, we might as well just let him reinvent the English language his way. We can all speak Alien instead of English. The two are very similar — one is just stupid.

Oh, and people started calling Mairi "Mighty Mike's Girlfriend" again. Of course.

In the meantime, the Mad Mask's ebony-and-ivory mask (now pocked with some dents and dings after the Army shot at me while I was wearing it) sits on a shelf in my basement next to the jar of radioactive dirt from Mighty Mike's landing site.

My workshop/laboratory is a mess. Most of my hard-earned materials were cannibalized to build Ultitron. The biochemical forge is useless, the chemicals inside it slowly turning inert as the days go by. Everything I've built since my intellect increased has been wrecked, destroyed.

But that's all right. I can rebuild. I will rebuild.

Whatever it takes.

I'll say this:

I am more determined than ever before to destroy Mighty Mike. If he had focused on the Mad Mask instead of me, Ultitron never would have been a threat.

If he hadn't distracted me by fighting me at Lundergaard, I could have stopped the Mad Mask sooner and none of this ever would have happened. Mairi wouldn't have been kidnapped, Ultitron wouldn't have been activated . . . None of it.

Someday the world will know the truth about him.

Most important, someday Mairi will know.

This I swear.

EPILOGUE

It took days of wandering the sewers before he eventually emerged.

Without a compass or a map or any sort of assistance, he had wandered in circles, trudging through disgusting rivers of slime and muck. He caught and ate rats, drank condensation that collected along the ceiling. It made him ill, but illness would not stop him. Being sick was for lesser beings, not for the likes of the Mad Mask.

He finally came out of the sewers into the cool night air for the first time since unleashing Ultitron on the world.

The sewer conduit emptied out on the outskirts of Bouring. Looking back, the Mad Mask could see that the town was being rebuilt. But it would take time for the damage to be repaired, and even longer for the memories to fade. Beautiful little Bouring would be frightening and ugly for a long time.

The Mad Mask took a piece of wet cardboard, poked two holes in it, and strung a shoelace through it, then slipped it over his head. He had to cover his disfigure-ment from the world. Until the day that the entire world was as hideous as he was.

And that day *would* come! He swore it! He would have his revenge. Not just on the beautiful things in the world. No, not just the beautiful things. He would have his revenge on Mighty Mike, too.

And on . . . on . . .

He couldn't remember entirely. But he knew there had been a traitor. Someone had betrayed him, stabbed him in the back and stolen his true face.

"The Mad Mask shall rise again!" he chortled to the sky. "The Mad Mask will have his revenge upon the trai-tor! Upon the Blue Freak!"

And he ran off into the darkness, his maniacal laugh following him.

Next in

ARCHVILLAiN

Kyle finally travels through time, journeying to the past to learn the truth about what happened the night Mighty Mike came to Earth. . . .

ACKNOWLEDGMENTS

Thanks to everyone at Scholastic, who continue to make working on Archvillain more fun than should be legal. Special thanks to Jody Corbett, David Levithan, and editor emeritus Gregory Rutty.

A hearty plasma-powered shout-out of thanks, too, to my beta readers: Eric Lyga, Faith Hochhalter, and Mary Kole. You are all as wise as Erasmus (and, when I need it, as snarky) and as cuddly as Lefty.

ABOUT THE AUTHOR

Barry Lyga is the author *Archvillain*, the first novel of Kyle Camden's adventures. He's also the author of several critically acclaimed YA novels. Barry lives in Brooklyn, New York. When he's not writing he uses his superpowers to fight crime.